韋爾◎著

倍斯特出版事業有限公司
Best Publishing Ltd.

U0077361

每日一句的Instagram PO文

輕鬆學好英文寫作

獨一無二的Instagram英語體驗

28個英文句型＋**28**篇英文作文
＝魅力Instagram英語人氣王

四大用途
◎ 看懂**好萊塢巨星**最新的Instagram動態
◎ **即刻用英文發出**最新的動態
◎ 洋洋灑灑寫一篇**文情並茂**的英文文章
◎ 在各類英文測驗的寫作項目**拿高分**

五大特色
◎ **英文句型＋延伸**：一種句型×多種變化
◎ **句型小貼士**：詳盡的句型用法解說
　→ 看懂發文訊息，迅速掌握最新的動態情報

◎ **句型腦激盪**：提供多樣化的例句
◎ **短句變長句＋PO文小練習**
　→ 貼切地PO出最新的動態與親友、粉絲分享

◎ **作文範例及解析**中分享寫作的高分秘訣 → 句型簡單用、輕鬆學寫作

作者序
author

　　隨著智慧型手機的普及以及許多社群系統的開發，越來越多人也使用臉書或 Instagram 等上傳自己的相片或抒發自己的想法，其中也不乏許多人用英語表達自己的看法或感受，而此書包含了極為簡易的句型作為搭配，除了能以輕鬆的步調學習英語，更能現學現用將句型跟慣用語搭配 Instagram 照片一起使用，更替自己的臉書增添幾分色彩。

　　此外，本書每個句型還搭配了一篇作文，讀者能夠藉由作文話題引入自己的想法，由生活化作文題材引入自己的想法，將自己的想法用於英文寫作中，像是上傳一張夜市傳統美食照片的同時，與飲食題材的作文作為搭配，將自己的想法融入於考試中並寫出自己的獨特看法。

　　最後誠摯感謝出版社給與本人此次出書機會。

韋爾

編者序
Editor

你知道根據一項 2014 年年底的調查指出，Instagram 的活躍用戶數已超過了 3 億？而在 2014 年的下半年度，其活躍用戶數就成長了 62%，名列在 2014 年度成長最快的社交服務前三名嗎？那你還知道根據 Instagram 的統計，平均每一秒鐘就有超過 800 張的照片或是影片被上傳嗎？那你知道只要用在 Instagram 中出現的 PO 文簡單英語句型，就能寫出一篇洋洋灑灑、文情並茂的好文章嗎？

書中介紹了可以用在 Instagram 發文的簡單英語句型，教你看懂心目中男神、女神的 Instagram 發文，隨時 follow 流行教主 PO 出的最新消息，不用只靠著圖像而總是一知半解，還能靈活運用句型 PO 你的最新動態。另外提供了英文寫作範例，教你用簡單英語句型輕鬆寫出能在各項英文測驗中拿高分的文章。

請跟我們一起來學最 IN 的 Instagram 發文句型，隨時發出你的最新動態。也輕鬆地寫出文意通順的英文文章，在各式的英文測驗中過關斬將！

編輯群

目次
CONTENTS

Part 1
Instagram PO文＋寫作初級篇

Part 2

Instagram PO文＋寫作高級篇

Instagram

PO 文+寫作初級篇

可以這樣寫

1. There is no Photoshop in real life.
   現實生活中沒有 Photoshop。

2. There are gorgeous figurines on John's desk.
   約翰的桌上有華麗的小雕像。

句型小貼士

- There is/there are 為常用的基本句型，其句型後常接代名詞或名詞，在加上時間或地點。

- 否定詞 no/not 置於 there is/are 後，如例句 1 中，否定詞 no 置於 there is/are 後，表示沒有…。

- 形容詞修飾名詞，且置於 there is/are 和名詞中間，如例句 2 中 gorgeous 置於 there is/are 和 figurines 中間。

句型腦激盪

★There is a lake house.

⇨ There is a lake house near the suburb.

在郊區附近有一個湖邊小屋。

★There is a town.

⇨ There is a small town in this valley.

在這山谷裡有一個小鎮。

★There are clocks.

⇨ There are many clocks in the antique shop.

在古董店裡有許多的鐘。

★There are restaurants.

⇨ There are several restaurants in the city.

在這個城市裡有好幾家餐廳。

★There are bicycles.

⇨ There are a lot of free bicycles in the resort.

在度假村里有許多免費的腳踏車。

★There are amenities.

⇨ There are some less commonly available amenities in this hotel.

在這間飯店裡有一些比較不太常有的設施。

★There are recreational facilities.

⇨ There are new recreational facilities in that amusement park.

在那個遊樂場裡有新的娛樂設施。

★There are wild animals.

⇨There are many wild animals in this national park.
在這座國家公園裡有許多的野生動物。

★There are fruits.

⇨There are some fresh fruits in the cafeteria area.
在自助餐區有一些新鮮的水果。

★There are castles.

⇨There are hundreds of castles in the UK.
在英國有數百座的城堡。

Instagram PO 文小練習

Tips：你在哪裡看到了什麼呢？

There is / are _____

_____

作文範例

Junk food, such as Coke, French fries, fried chicken, and pearl milk tea is like a godsend, but governments are now starting to realize that it's a problem that needs to be solved instantly. Do you think it is fair for the government to impose tax on junk food?

1 In some developed countries, governments are adopting the idea of imposing a higher tax on junk food so that people can be partially immune from health-related diseases. Consumers are less likely to eat junk food if the price is relatively high or unreasonable, but for those who deem those junk foods as gourmet meals, imposing such tax is useless.

2 Most importantly, in Taiwan, walking down the street, we can find people waiting in line for the pearl milk tea, but that is not all. They prefer to drink pearl milk tea, while having fried chickens and French fries, and so on. They have become addicted to these foods. Addiction to these foods has aggravated people's overall health according to the survey, but people will not think it is a problem until they encounter physical problems.

3 From my viewpoint, I do think governments should take other measures to control the situation, imposing the tax, even though it seems reasonable, is useless. After all, it is their choice of food, and why should governments step in? Moreover, there are still other street peddlers who are not in the norm of the stipulation, and most people can still buy junk foods from the night market. Also, it is highly unlikely for government to go door to door and regulate their citizens from having the French fries if those citizens buy potatoes and want to cook that way. It is people's choice of cooking every meal. Even if legalized, it will only affect the fast food industry which sells those junk foods to citizens, but it will not be a problem for people who buy chickens and want to fry them at home.

4 In conclusion, higher tax imposition will not be the solution to the problem, since there is always a need. Governments should think other ways instead of simply imposing the higher tax.

作文中譯加解析

Unit 1
Unit 2
Unit 3
Unit 4
Unit 5
Unit 6
Unit 7
Unit 8
Unit 9
Unit 10
Unit 11
Unit 12
Unit 13
Unit 14
Unit 15

　　垃圾食物像是可樂、薯條、炸雞和珍珠奶茶就像是天降之禮，但是政府現在正體認到這是需要即刻解決的問題。你認為課垃圾食物稅是否真的能解決問題嗎？

1 在許多已開發國家，政府對垃圾食物正採用了課較高額的稅的想法，所以人們能部分地免於相關疾病的困擾。消費者較不可能吃垃圾食品，如果價格相對來說較高或不合理，但對於將垃圾食物視為美食的人來説，課稅根本沒有用。

- 首段先引入主題，説明現況，並提出這個政策有用及沒有用的原因為何。

2 最重要的是在台灣，走在街上幾乎隨處可見人們排隊買珍珠奶茶，且現象不只如此。他們喜歡飲用珍珠奶茶時，搭配炸雞和薯條等食物。對垃圾食物成癮，且根據調查對垃圾食物成癮使民眾的整體健康惡化了，但是人們直到身體出狀況了才驚覺這個問題。

- 第二段説明飲食習慣跟原因，舉出相關證明，及垃圾食物對身體的危害。

3 我認為政府應採用其他措施控制此情況，課稅即使看似合理，卻無法解決問題。畢竟，這是人們自己的選擇，政府為什麼要干涉？此外，仍有其他街販不會在規範內，人們仍可以從夜市中買到此類的垃圾食品。而且，政府幾乎不可能挨家挨戶的規範市民，規範其不能炸薯條，如果他們買馬鈴薯且要以此方式烹煮。這是民眾烹煮食物的選擇，且即使合法化，也只影響到買垃圾食物給市民的速食業者，但不會影響到買雞肉且要在家炸的人。

- 第三段說明自己的觀點，以 From my viewpoint 開頭，列舉出自己的看法，並提出一些為什麼課徵重稅並無法解決這一個問題的例子。

4 結論是，高額的課稅並不是解決之道，且總是會有需求在。政府應該要想其他方法，而非僅僅是課高額的稅。

- 最後以 In conclusion 做總結，呼應前三段中所寫的部分，做簡短的結論，完結這一篇文章。

字彙補一補

1. immune **adj.** 免疫的，免於⋯的
   We are immune from the torture of Professor John's lecture.
   我們對於約翰教授的授課折磨已經免疫了。

2. gourmet **n.** 美食
   Having a gourmet meal after work is a must.
   工作後享用美食是必須的。

3. aggravate **v.** 加重、使惡化
   It will certainly aggravate your kidney function.
   這肯定會使你的腎功能惡化。

4. stipulation **n.** 契約、規定、條文
   The stipulation is hard to read.
   這條文很難讀懂。

5. regulate **v.** 管理、控制
   It is hard to regulate those who tend to break the rule.
   很難去規範那些傾向打破規則的人。

6. legalize **v.** 使⋯合法
   Whether gay marriage will be legalized or not still varies from countries to countries.
   同性婚姻是否合法，仍然因每個國家而有所不同。

| **重點解析**

1. In some developed countries, governments are adopting to impose a higher tax on junk food so that people can be partially immune from health-related diseases.

   在許多已開發國家，政府對垃圾食物正採用了課較高額的稅，所以人們能部分地免於相關疾病的困擾。

   > • governments are adopting to…用現在進行式，表示政府正採用…。
   > • to impose a higher tax…為不定詞 to+impose，表示課較高額的稅。
   > • so that…表示如此以致於…
   > • be immune from…表示…使…免於，句中加上副詞 partially，表示能部分免於…。

2. Consumers are less likely to eat junk food if the price is relatively high or unreasonable, but for those who deem those junk foods as gourmet, imposing such tax is useless.

   消費者較不可能吃垃圾食品，如果價格相對來説較高或不合理，但對於將垃圾食物視為美食的人來説，課稅根本沒有用。

   > • are less likely…表示較不可能…。
   > • if…表示條件句引導一副詞子句，為 if+S+V 的句型。
   > • but 為對等連接詞，其後加上 but for those…表示對那些…來説，表示相反的語意。

3. Addiction to these foods has aggravated people's overall health according to the survey, but people will not think it is a problem until they encounter physical problems.

根據調查對垃圾食物成癮使民眾的整體健康惡化了，但是人們直到身體出了狀況才驚覺這個問題。

- according to 表示根據…，常置於句首其後加上逗號，文中為 according to the survey 表示根據調查。
- Addiction to these foods has aggravated people's over-all health 中，由 addiction 當主詞，**has aggravated** 用完成式表示已使得…，句中表示已使得人們整體健康惡化。
- **but** 為對等連接詞，表示語意的轉折，句中表示人們直到發現身體出發狀況才意識到這是個問題。**Until** 表示直到…。

one of
其中之一

可以這樣寫

/////////////

1. One of the most memorable views is the waterfall.
   最值得懷念的景色之一是瀑布。

2. One of the worthwhile parts for visiting the zoo is the chance of getting photos with favorite animals.
   參觀動物園最值得的部分之一是有機會與最喜愛的動物拍照。

句型小貼士

- one of… 表示「其中之一」，為常用的基本句型，of 後加複數名詞，但主詞是 one 故其後加單數動詞，在寫作跟答文法題時要特別小心。

- 例 2 作了延伸，在複數名詞後加了介系詞片語 for visiting the zoo，the chance of getting photos 為拍照的機會，其後加 with…表示「與…」，句中指的是 with favorite animals。

[⚡] 句型腦激盪

/////////////

★One of the most memorable views is the waterfall.
⇨One of the most memorable views is the waterfall on the hill.
最值得懷念的景色之一是在峭壁上的瀑布。

★One of the most attractive things is insects.
⇨One of the most attractive things is euphonious sounds of the insects.
最吸引人的事之一是昆蟲悦耳的聲音。

★One of the most reminiscent views is traditional buildings.
⇨One of the most reminiscent views is remarkable traditional buildings.
最值得回憶的景色之一是著名的傳統建築物。

★One of the most remarkable views is flowers.
⇨One of the most remarkable views is rare flowers on the cliff.
最著名的景色之一是懸崖上罕見的花。

★One of the most beautiful views is trees.
⇨One of the most beautiful views is trees with a giant stature.
最美麗的景色之一是有巨大形態的樹。

★One of the most memorable views is the lake.
⇨One of the most memorable views is the lake that gives us peace.
最值得懷念的景色之一是能帶給我們平和感的湖泊。

★One of the most lingering views is salmons.

⇨One of the most lingering views is salmons in the river.

最令人流連忘返的景色之一是在河裡的鮭魚。

★One of the most charming views is koalas.

⇨One of the most charming views is koalas on the tree.

最令人感到有魅力的景色之一是在樹上的無尾熊。

★One of the most memorable views is gazelles.

⇨One of the most memorable views is gazelles on the grass.

最令人嚮往的景色之一是在草地上的羚羊。

★One of the most agreeable views is elephants.

⇨One of the most agreeable views is elephants exhibiting powers.

最宜人的景色之一是展示出力量的大象。

Instagram PO文小練習

Tips：要記得這一句後面要放複數的名詞！

One of _____

_____

作文範例

People seem to have a different point of view when it comes to work. People used to work for the same organization all their working life, but nowadays this has not been the case. People of our generation change their jobs very often. This is contrary to what is on HR executives' mind, for three years of working for the same organization are the minimum of accumulating work experiences in specific areas. What is your opinion of this phenomenon?

1 Nowadays, with changes in attitude, most people will not work for the same organization all their working life. Sometimes it really varies from place to place and factors that are attributed to work for the same organization or different organizations are complicated and cannot be quantified.

2 For some people, there is nothing wrong working in the same organization all their working life, especially the government institution even if they have to do the same thing over and over. For people working in the public sectors, they will have a stable life with only eight working hours per day. For people who are reluctant to change, working in the same organization is absolutely a paradise, and boredom is not in their vocabulary at all. After all, changes in workplace

21

are the only threat and <u>one of</u> the primary considerations for quitting the job.

3 However, other than personality and other factors, there are still benefits for people who change their jobs. When people work for the same organization for three years, they have become familiar with how the company operates and have packaged with adequate knowledge and expertise for the position. If they have demonstrated outstanding performances in the job, they are likely to be promoted internally. It is also the time for them to leave because there are other jobs out there. This will also be a defining moment for them exploring outside world and learn a range of skills and experience in different organizations.

4 From the above, it is really varies from person to person because it is their own career. To me, working in the different organization outweighs working in the same organization simply because I am a lifelong learner. It will certainly give me some incentives to learn and ultimately reach my career goal.

作文中譯加解析

　　人們似乎在講到工作時都會有不同的看法。以前人們多會一直待在同一家公司工作，但是在現今社會中卻不再如此。我們這一個世代的人常常會換工作。這與人事主管的想法是相悖而行的，因為對於某些特別的領域而言，待在同一家公司工作最少要三年才能累積足夠的工作經驗。你對於這一種現象的看法是什麼呢？

1 在現今的社會，隨著態度的改變，大多數的人不會在工作生涯中一直都待在同一個機構。有時候，可能會因為工作的單位不一樣而有所不同。而一直待在同一家公司或是不同公司的因素是極其複雜且無法量化的。

- 首段指出題目中所述的待在同一家，或是不同家公司，在現在的社會中，因為態度的改變，所以大多數人不再會一直待在同一家公司，但也說明這一個問題牽扯到許多因素，所以是複雜。

2 對某些人來說，終其一生在相同機構工作並沒有什麼不好，尤其像是在公家機構工作的人，儘管是每天都要一直重複相同的工作。對在公家單位工作的人而言，這是一份一天 8 小時且能帶來安穩生活的工作。對於不想改變的人來說，在相同機構工作絕對像是宛如置身天堂一般，且沉悶感絕不會存在在他們的感受裡。畢竟工作環境的改變才是唯一的威脅，且為辭職的主因之一。

- 第二段包含了三句論述分別由 for some people、for people working in the public sectors 和 for people who are reluctant to change，分別說明了會待在相同機構工作的原因。

3 然而,除了是性格或是其他的原因之外,對於換工作的人而言還是
   有一些益處。對於在相同機構工作三年的人來說,他們已經熟悉公
   司的運作且具備了此職務所需的足夠知識和專長。如果他們在此工
   作中表現傑出,他們可能會於內部中晉升。而這也是他們轉換跑道
   的時機。這也是他們的關鍵時期,探索外面的世界,從其他公司中
   學習不同範圍的技巧和經驗。

   • 以 however 開頭表示轉折,說明除了個性和其他因素轉換工作
     對人們來說是有益處的(work for different organizations)。

4 從上面所說的,這應該是因人而異,畢竟這是他們個人的職涯規
   劃。對我而言在不同公司工作勝過終其一生待在同間公司工作,因
   為我是個終生學習者。而這將會使我有學習的誘因且最終達到我的
   目標。

   • 最後以 From the above 做總結,為重述法的使用,用上面幾段
     的說明來解釋對每個人來說應該會有所不同。這樣的題目本就是
     各有不同的支持論調,所以在前面先鋪陳利弊,最後闡述自己的
     主張。

字彙補一補

1. attribute **v.** 把…歸因於

The problems of lung cancer are attributed to the second-hand smoke.

肺炎的問題歸因於二手菸。

2. institution **n.** 機構

ABC Music is an institution of a high learning.

ABC 音樂是一所高等學習機構。

3. paradise **n.** 天堂

This is certainly a paradise for tree frogs.

這對樹蛙來說確實是個天堂。

4. demonstrate **v.** 證實。

This has demonstrated the fact that caffeine does offset the medication.

這已經被證實了，咖啡因會抵消了藥效。

5. outstanding **adj.** 傑出的

The doctor is very outstanding.

這個醫生很傑出。

6. outweigh **v.** 勝過

The benefit of working with you outweighs the benefit of working with others.

與你合作的利益勝過與其他人合作的利益。

重點解析

1. For people who are reluctant to change, working in the same organization is absolutely a paradise.

   對於不想改變的人來説，在相同機構工作絕對像是宛如置身天堂一般。

   - 整句為 for people⋯, S+V⋯。
   - be reluctant to 為不情願⋯。
   - working in the same organization is absolutely a paradise，為動名詞當主詞，故加單數動詞 is。

2. However, other than personality and other factors, there are still benefits for people who change their jobs.

   然而，除了是性格或是其他的原因之外，對於換工作的人而言還是有一些益處。

   - however 表語氣轉折⋯表示然而。
   - other than 表示除了⋯，句中表示除了個性和其他因素。
   - There is/there are 為常用的基本句型，其句型後常接代名詞或名詞，再加上時間或地點。
   - who 引導關係代名詞子句，句中為 who change their jobs 表示改變工作的人。

3. If they have demonstrated outstanding performances in the job, they are likely to be promoted internally.

如果他們在此工作中表現傑出，他們可能會於內部中晉升。

- if… 表示條件句引導一副詞子句，為 if+S+V 的句型。
- if they have demonstrated outstanding performances in the job，由 they 當主詞，has demonstrated 用完成式表示已展現出…，句中表示已於工作中展現傑出的表現。
- are likely to 表示可能…，其後加 to be promoted internally 表示於內部升遷。

Unit 3 fascinated by 為…著迷

可以這樣寫

//////////

1. Fascinated by the food, he has become a fan of that shop.

   為食物所著迷,他已成了該家店的粉絲了。

2. Fascinated by the scenery of the serene lake, he has an urge to draw it.

   為寧靜的湖泊景色感到著迷,他有股想畫圖的衝動。

句型小貼士

- fascinated by 為…著迷…為過去分詞構句,是常用的基本句型,其中 by 為介系詞,故其後加名詞或名詞片語。

- 過去分詞構句為過去分詞+…, S+V…的句型。

- 例句 1 中,僅僅於 fascinated by 加上 the food,例 2 後加了較長的名詞片語 the scenery of the serene lake。

⚡ 句型腦激盪

★Fascinated by the food, he has become a fan of that shop.

⇨Fascinated by the exotic flavor of the food, he has become a fan of that shop.

為異國風味食物所著迷，他已成了該家店的粉絲了。

★Fascinated by country music, he goes to that club four times per week.

⇨Fascinated by country music in the club, he goes to that club four times per week.

為俱樂部裡的鄉村音樂所著迷，他每四週光顧一次那家俱樂部。

★Fascinated by a small town, he bought a lake house immediately.

⇨Fascinated by a small town in the countryside, he bought a lake house immediately.

為鄉村裡的小鎮所著迷，他立即買了湖邊小屋。

★Fascinated by seafood, he has become a frequent visitor.

⇨Fascinated by seafood in the restaurant, he has become a frequent visitor.

為店裡的海鮮所著迷，他已成了該家店的常客了。

★Fascinated by fresh vegetables, he tells his neighbors that he wants some.

⇨Fascinated by fresh vegetables in the neighbor's yard, he tells his neighbors that he wants some.

為鄰居院子裡的新鮮蔬果所著迷，他告訴他的鄰居他想要一些。

★Fascinated by fruits, he climbs to the top of the tree.

⇨Fascinated by fruits of the giant tree, he climbs to the top of the tree.

為巨樹上的水果所著迷,他爬到樹頂端。

★Fascinated by honey, he starts to raise a colony.

⇨Fascinated by honey gathered by bees, he starts to raise a colony.

為蜂蜜所採的蜜所著迷,他開始養一群。

★Fascinated by fish, he takes pictures frames after frames.

⇨Fascinated by fish under the torrent, he takes pictures frames after frames.

為急流下的魚所著迷,他一張接著一張地拍照。

★Fascinated by ice cream, Jenny is reluctant to leave.

⇨Fascinated by ice cream in Ice Castle, Jenny is reluctant to leave.

為 Ice Castle 的冰淇淋所著迷,珍妮不願意離開。

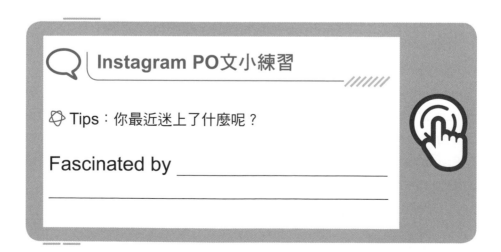

Instagram PO文小練習

Tips:你最近迷上了什麼呢?

Fascinated by _____

_____

作文範例

///////////

There are other alternatives for either going to work or travelling to the destination. A combination of several public transportation facilities, such as MRT, BRT, and U-bike, is the new trend, but governments are still trying to figure how to solve the traffic jam problems. What do you think about this phenomenon?

1 Fascinated by the advantages of having one's cars, there is no denying that having a car of your own is certainly more convenient and time-saving. They can enjoy the comfort of not cramming into the bus or enjoy their own freedom and space. Sometimes it is not convenient for us to take the public transportation if you have kids or have to take the elderly to other places. All these things are contributing to the traffic jam problems over the past thirty years.

2 With lots of transportation facilities, such as MRT, BRT, and other means of transportation being built, people are more willing to take public transportations. It is more convenient than driving you cars in the peak time while still struggling to find the place to park in the city. Moreover, sometimes even if it is not in the peak time, traffic problems persist.

Unit 1
Unit 2
Unit 3
Unit 4
Unit 5
Unit 6
Unit 7
Unit 8
Unit 9
Unit 10
Unit 11
Unit 12
Unit 13
Unit 14
Unit 15

3 Encouragement of using the public transport is the approach most cities adopt, but there are other things our government can do. Other than the encouragement of using public transport, people now can take U-bike to the destination whether they are heading to work or school. A combination of taking the MRT first and having the U-bike is the most popular way for most Taipei citizens. Also, the commute time can be saved. This is the successful example of combining several transport facilities.

4 Another thing that our government can do is to build the ring-like MRT for commuters and independent rails for bicycle riders. People taking erected ring-like MRT can reach their destination by having fewer than five or seven stations than they used to, while people taking independent rails can enjoy the scenery without driving the vehicle.

5 To sum up, efforts have been made from many city mayors, and as a citizen it is also our responsibility to find other alternatives, such as carpooling or taking the U-bike, so that traffic jam problems can be solved.

作文中譯加解析

Unit 1
Unit 2
Unit 3
Unit 4
Unit 5
Unit 6
Unit 7
Unit 8
Unit 9
Unit 10
Unit 11
Unit 12
Unit 13
Unit 14
Unit 15

　　對於去上班或到某個目的地旅行，有了其他的替代方案。幾個大眾運輸設施的結合，例如 MRT, BRT 和 U-bike 等等，是個新的趨勢，但政府仍試著找出解決交通擁擠問題的方法。你對這個現象的想法是什麼呢？

1 被擁有自己的一輛車的優點所吸引，其無法否認的是擁有自己的車的確是更便利而且是更省時的。可以享有不必擠在巴士裡的舒適感或是能享有個人自由和空間。如果隨行的人員中有孩童或是必須帶家中的老人到某個地方，有些時候，搭乘大眾交通工具對我們而言並不是那樣地便利。而以上這些因素，都導致了過去三十年間交通擁擠的問題。

- 首段先引入主題，先說明大多數人無法否認擁有自己的車是便利且省時的。並提出擁有自己的車子的優點，而這也是造成題目中「交通擁擠」的原因。

2 隨著多種大眾運輸設施，例如 MRT、BRT 和其他交通工具的興建，人們更願意搭乘大眾運輸設施。在市區尖峰時刻時，搭乘大眾運輸較自己開車更為方便且不用煩惱找停車位。此外，有時候儘管是於非尖峰時刻，仍有交通擁擠的問題。

- 下段說明，各式大眾交通工具的興建完成讓人們更傾向於搭乘大眾運輸工具，基於所提出的幾項優點。

3 鼓勵使用大眾運輸是大多數城市所採用的方法，但是我們政府仍有其他方法可以應對。除了鼓勵使用大眾運輸之外，人們現在可於上班或工作時騎乘 U-bike 抵達目的地。以先搭乘 MRT 再改以 U-bike 的方式，是許多台北市民所採用的方式。也能省下許多通勤的時間。這就是一個成功的結合搭乘大眾運輸的例子。

- 這一段以成功例子來舉例，先舉出其他大多數城市所採用的方法，但是我們政府有其他的應對方式，以已施行成功的大眾運輸結合方案為例以強化論點。

4 政府還能採行的其他可行方法有為通勤族興建環狀捷運系統和獨立的單車道。人們搭乘已興建的環狀捷運系統，能比過去搭乘捷運時，節省搭乘五至七站。人們使用為自行車者興建獨立的單車道，能不用開車就能沿途觀賞風景。

- 再補充除了其他可施行方案以及這些方案的優點。

5 總結以上的論點，顯示出許多市長都做了許多的努力，而身為市民的我們有責任要去找出其他替代方案，例如汽車共乘或搭乘 U-bike，交通擁擠的問題才能獲得解決。

- 最後以總結短語 "to sum up" 來做為總結，to sum up 為衍生法的使用，這後面接上認可許多市長之前所推行的解決方案，並從自身為市民的觀點來說，也應該負起解決交通擁擠的問題，能從找出適合的方案開始。

字彙補一補

1. contribute **v.** 促成；捐獻
Contributing half of one's money to the charity is noble.
捐出半數金錢給慈善機構是很高尚的。

2. encouragement **n.** 鼓勵
Encouragement is perhaps one of the best ways in teaching.
鼓勵或許是教學中最好的方法之一。

3. destination **n.** 目的地
The next destination is thrilling.
下個目的地令人感到興奮。

4. independent **adj.** 獨立的
The independent amusement park is the main attraction.
這一獨立的遊樂園是主要的景點。

5. scenery **n.** 景色
The scenery is beyond our imagination.
景色超乎我們的想像。

6. alternative **n.** 替代方案
XYZ company always has other alternatives when facing shipping problems.
面臨運輸問題時，XYZ 公司總是有其他的替代方案。

重點解析

1. Encouragement of using the public transport is the approach most cities adopt, but there are other things our government can do.

   鼓勵使用大眾運輸是大多數城市所採用的方法，但是我們政府仍有其他方法可以應對。

   - encouragement 當主詞，動詞為 is。
   - but 為對等連接詞，表示相反的語意。
   - There is/there are 為常用的基本句型，其句型後常接代名詞或名詞，再加上時間或地點。

2. Another thing that our government can do is to build the ring-like MRT for commuters and independent rails for bicycle riders.

   政府還能採行的其他可行方法有為通勤族興建環狀捷運系統和獨立的單車道。

   - Another thing that our government can do is… 表列舉，表示政府能作了另一件事是…。
   - the ring-like MRT for commuters and independent rails for bicycle riders，以對等連接詞連接，for 則清楚表明對象分別是 commuters 和 bicycle riders。

3. People taking erected ring-like MRT can reach their destination by having fewer than five or seven stations than they used to, while people taking independent rails can enjoy the scenery without driving the vehicle.

人們搭乘已興建的環狀捷運系統，能比過去搭乘捷運時，節省搭乘五至七站。人們使用為自行車者興建獨立的單車道，能不用開車就能沿途觀賞風景。

- People taking 為關係代名詞子句省略 people who take，主要動詞是 can reach，句中表示人們搭乘建好的環狀捷運…。
- By+ving 表示藉由…，句中表示比之前少了五至七站。
- than 為比較級表程度，文中為 than they used to 表示比他們之前更…。
- while 為對等連接詞，表示語意的轉折，連接兩句子，而兩句都以 people taking 為開頭…。
- enjoy 後面加 Ving，而 without 為介詞其後亦加名詞或 Ving。

Unit 4 sitting in/on
坐在…

可以這樣寫

//////////

1. Sitting in the dreamy coffee shop with hazelnut latte and Tiramisu sounds like a perfect way to spend a Sunday afternoon.

   坐在夢幻咖啡店有著榛果拿鐵和提拉米蘇，聽起來像是度過週日下午最理想的方式。

2. Sitting in the roller coaster with your friends sounds like a wild way to spend your weekend.

   與朋友們乘坐雲霄飛車，聽起來像是度過你的週末最瘋狂的方式。

句型小貼士

• Sitting in/on… 坐在…，為動名詞當主詞，是常用的基本句型，其中需注意加單數動詞，為許多考試常考句型，注意勿被離動詞較近的名詞干擾到。

• 動名詞的句型為 V-ing…+單數動詞的句型。

• 例句 1 與例句 2 僅差在 sitting 後地點跟乘坐的東西的不同，而 sounds like 為聽起來像是…，為極常見的用語。

句型腦激盪

★Sitting in the gym sounds like a perfect way to spend a national holiday.

⇨Sitting in the gym with the flag of your country sounds like a perfect way to spend a national holiday.

坐在體育館有著你自己國家的旗子，聽起來像是度過一個國定假日最理想的方式。

★Sitting in the movie theater sounds like a perfect way to spend a Sunday afternoon.

⇨Sitting in the movie theater with your girl friends sounds like a perfect way to spend a Sunday afternoon.

與女性友人們坐在電影院，聽起來像是度過週日下午最理想的方式。

★Sitting in the art museum sounds like a perfect way to spend a Sunday afternoon.

⇨Sitting in the art museum hall to have a cup of coffee sounds like a perfect way to spend a Sunday afternoon.

坐在藝術博物館享用一杯咖啡，聽起來像是度過週日下午最理想的方式。

★Sitting in the concert hall sounds like a perfect way to spend a Sunday afternoon.

⇨Sitting in the concert hall which was designed by a famous architect sounds like a perfect way to spend a Sunday afternoon.

坐在極富盛名的建築師所設計的音樂廳裡，聽起來像是度過週日下午最理想的方式。

★Sitting in the Italian coffee shop sounds like a perfect way to spend an afternoon.

⇨Sitting in the Italian coffee shop with an old-fashioned design sounds like a perfect way to spend a drowsy afternoon.

坐在具傳統設計的義式咖啡館內，聽起來像是度過令人昏昏欲睡的下午最理想的方式。

★Sitting in the Spa sounds like a perfect way to spend a summer day.

⇨Sitting in the Spa with mineral-rich water sounds like a perfect way to spend a hot summer day.

坐在具富含礦物質水源的 Spa，聽起來像是度過週日下午最理想的方式。

★Sitting in the stir fry restaurants with friends sounds like a perfect way to spend a Saturday night.

⇨Sitting in the stir fry restaurants with your good friends sounds like a perfect way to spend a Saturday night.

與朋友坐在快炒店，聽起來像是度過星期六晚上最理想的方式。

Instagram PO文小練習

Tips：你坐在那裡有了怎樣的體驗呢？

Sitting in _____

_____

作文範例

Thanks to health care and improved medical device, our life expectancy has increased significantly during the past decades, but some people are starting to have a concern of this phenomenon. What is your opinion?

1 When <u>sitting on</u> the hospital bench with your relatives to think about the progress of the improved medical care is the time for us to realize the fact that with the improved medical care, people now live longer than they used to. On the surface, it is a good thing for all of us, but the underlying problem is severe and complicated.

2 When people are living longer, social problems are bigger. There should be lots of care and support from either the government or the family. Across all countries, there is a shortage of birth for new-borne babies, which means there is a lack of adequate workforce for the entire society to back up the cost of taking good care of the elderly. Moreover, the problem seems to be a lot worse than it appears. In most countries, most young people can barely make a living let alone taking good care of their family members and the elderly.

3 For elder people, whether they are healthy or not, they will be given monthly payment and several other things from the government, and this is a huge social cost. Elder people who have saved enough even if they do not have kids can live a relatively well life after their retirement, but for those who do not, they will have a rough life in their sixties and seventies. Sometimes they are even forced to work because they still have a grandkid to look after. For the unhealthy elderly, they can be a great burden for the family. Even some are entirely dependent on others from eating to bathing.

4 To sum up, I think people should start as early as possible to carefully plan their retired life so that they do not have to rely on their kids or others. Also, people should have a healthy lifestyle and exercise regularly so that they can truly enjoy their retirement, and living longer can be advantageous to our society.

作文中譯加解析

> 　　多虧了健康照護和進步的醫療裝置，我們壽命在過去幾十年已經大幅地增加，但有些人對這現象已開始有所擔憂。你的看法是？

1　當與親戚坐在醫院板凳上思考著醫療問題時，我們瞭解到一項事實，隨著醫療照護的進步，人們現在活得比之前更久了。表面上來說，對我們而言是件好事，但其潛在的問題卻是很嚴重且複雜的。

- 首段先引入主題，先說明隨著醫療照護的進步，所以造成人的壽命變長。進而剖析利弊，以表面上（**on the surface**）加上潛在的（**underlying**）來說，營造出有一體兩面的感覺，由此帶出事情的優、缺點。

2　當人們活得更久，社會問題更大。且政府或家庭也需要更多的照護和支持。對所有國家來說，都面臨了新生嬰兒數的短少，這也意謂著整個社會缺乏足夠的人力去支持照護好老年人的開支。且此問題也比所表現出來的問題更為嚴重。在大多數的國家，年輕人僅能勉強維持生計，更別說是要照顧好他們的家庭成員和老年人。

- 此段承接上段所說的，針對潛在的問題作闡述。先說明當人們活得更久，社會問題更大。並分成兩個部分來解釋。第一個是低出生率相對地造成的社會勞動力斷層的問題，而人的壽命增加也意味著需要照護的需求以及人利的增加。第二個是從經濟層面來看，許多國家年輕人的收入不足以照顧好家中老人。

43

3 對老年人而言，無論其是否健康，政府會給予每月的補助和幾個其他照護項目，這其實是巨大的社會成本。對於存夠退休所需的老年人，即使他們沒有小孩仍然在退休後，可以享有相當好的退休生活。但是對於那些沒有存夠退休所需的老年人，他們將會面臨在六十和七十幾歲的更困苦的生活。有時會因為有孫子要照顧而被迫就業。對於那一些身體不好的老年人而言，他們會成為家中的負擔。甚至有些從吃東西到洗澡都全然仰賴他人照護。

• 這段將老年人在退休後的情形以兩個分類（存夠退休所需及沒有存夠的）分別闡述，兩句之間以 but 表轉折，用以形容兩種完全不同的情況。並提出可能會因此有再度就業的現象。而後半段則是討論身體不好的老年人，因會有照料的問題，呼應上一段所提到的部分。

4 作為總結，我認為人們應更早且謹慎規劃其退休生活，所以他們不用全然仰賴他們自己小孩或其他人。而且，人們應有健康的生活習慣，規律地運動才能真正享有他們退休的生活，而社會也能因人們活得更久而受益。

• 最後以 to sum up 作為總結語，並說明自己觀點，以上面幾段所提到的問題，追本溯源至解決這一些問題的根本，以規劃退休生活、養成良好的習慣等，我們才能在老年時過更好及有尊嚴的生活。

字彙補一補

1. underlying **adj.** 潛在的
The underlying problem cannot be easily solved.
潛在的問題並不容易解決。

2. shortage **n.** 短缺
There is a shortage of students in rural elementary schools.
鄉村小學出現學生短缺。

3. entire **adj.** 全然的
This is not entirely her fault.
這不全然是她的錯。

4. rough **adj.** 粗糙的
The surface of the basketball is rough.
籃球的表面是粗糙的。

5. regularly **adj.** 定期地
Exercising regularly is very important.
定期地運動是非常重要的。

6. advantageous **adj.** 有利的
It will be advantageous to our firm if we eventually get the contract from ABC company.
這將會對我們公司有利，如果我們最終能談成與 ABC 公司合約的話。

45

重點解析

1. With the improved medical care, people now live longer than they used to.

隨著醫療照護的進步，人們現在活的比之前更久了。

- With 為介系詞表示隨著…。
- used to 表示過去是…。
- with the improved medical care 表示隨著醫療照護的進步。
- live longer than they used to 表示活的比之前更久了，比較級時常用 than 作搭配。

2. In most countries, most young people can barely make a living let alone taking good care of their family members and the elderly.

在大多數的國家，年輕人僅能勉強維持生計，更別說是要照顧好他們的家庭成員和老年人。

- In most countries 表示在大多數的國家。
- barely make a living 表示僅能勉強餬口…。
- let alone 表示更別說是…。
- take care of 表示照顧…

3. For elder people, whether they are healthy or not, they will be given monthly payment and several other things from the government, and this is a huge social cost.

對老年人來説，不管他們是否健康，他們每個月都會從政府那裡獲得補助和許多其他東西，而這是巨額的社會成本。

- For elder people 表示對老年人來説…。
- whether 表示是否…引導一名詞子句，其句型為 Whether+S+V，S+V。
- will be given monthly payment and several other things from the government 表示每個月都會從政府那裡獲得補助和許多其他東西，其中 will be given 表被動式。
- and 為對等連接詞連接兩句子。

since (one's salad days) 自從…（年少不更事的時期）

 可以這樣寫

1. Since his salad days, his rebellious personality has not changed a bit.

   自從他年少不更事的時期，他叛逆的性格未曾有一絲改變。

2. Since her salad days, Susan's viewpoint towards love hasn't changed.

   自從她年少不更事的時期，蘇珊對愛的看法未曾改變過。

句型小貼士

- Since 表示自…以來，是常用的基本句型，在句型中使用廣泛，能當句中連接詞和介系詞等功用。

- one's salad days… 指某個人年少不更事的時期/剛初出茅廬的時期。

⚡ 句型腦激盪

★Since his salad days, his personality has not changed a bit.

⇨Since his salad days, his rebellious personality has not changed a bit.

自從他年少不更事的時期，他叛逆的性格未曾有一絲改變。

★Since Mary's salad days, her attitude has not changed a bit.

⇨Since Mary's salad days, her attitude towards money has not changed a bit.

從 Mary 年少不更事的時期，她對金錢的態度未曾有一絲改變。

★Since Janet's salad days, her value has changed a bit.

⇨Since Janet's salad days, her value towards parenting has changed a bit.

自從 Janet 年少不更事的時期，她對養育子女的價值未曾有一絲改變。

★Since his salad days, his stereotype has not changed a bit.

⇨Since his salad days, his gender stereotype has not changed a bit.

自從他年少不更事的時期，他的性別刻板印象未曾有一絲改變。

★Since his salad days, he has dreamed of working in the Disneyland.

⇨Since his salad days, he has dreamed of working in the Disneyland one day.

自從他年少不更事的時期，他已夢想著能在迪士尼樂園工作。

★Since her salad days, her passion has not changed a bit.

⇨Since her salad days, her passion towards publishing has not changed a bit.

自從她年少不更事的時期，她對出版業的熱情未曾有一絲改變。

★Since his salad days, his enthusiasm has not changed a bit.

⇨Since his salad days, his enthusiasm towards writing has not changed a bit.

自從他年少不更事的時期，他對寫作的熱忱未曾有一絲改變。

★Since her salad days, her dressing style has not changed a bit.

⇨Since her salad days, her horrible dressing style has not changed a bit.

自從她年少不更事的時期，她可怕的穿著風格未曾有一絲改變。

★Since his salad days, his fondness for sports has not changed a bit.

⇨Since his salad days, his fondness for sports has not changed even a little bit.

自從他年少不更事的時期，他對體育的喜愛未曾有一絲改變。

Instagram PO文小練習

🌀 Tips：是誰的青蔥年少呢？也可以只用 since，做介系詞使用，表「自從」，在 since 的後面接上名詞或是名詞片語即可。

Since _____ salad days, _____

作文範例

With more technological devices being developed, we are exposed to a dangerous world. Some people claim that crime rates will be significantly reduced, if we have more of these devices, such as security cameras. Others think it is not helpful, worrying that the development of the technology will lead to more problems than we can possibly think of. What is your opinion?

1 <u>Since our salad days,</u> advanced technology has provided us with lots of comfort and convenience, but the development of the advanced technology also has triggered several problems. One that is the most relevant to our life is our safety.

2 Almost everywhere, from campuses, office buildings, and every street, there are security cameras. From governments' perspective erected cameras are the efficient ways of reducing crimes to a certain extent. From most citizens, it is like a placebo that walking down the street is safe. Even if there is a break-in in our home, we can always track the record from the security camera and find the villains. But in what ways can governments and citizens guarantee the crime rate will be significantly reduced if security cameras are erected? In real life, if people intend to commit a crime, they will certainly do that. They can switch the camera into other directions and commit a crime. They will not care whether there is a security camera or not.

3 Also, there are other concerns. With the other device being developed, it is likely that people are exposed to a vulnerable environment. Without careful considerations, people using so-called social-networking sites are the most susceptible to the technology hazards. With their personal information being revealed, they are likely to be victims of the crime. For example, while sharing a photo of buying a BMW car on the Facebook stating that "just bought" or "it's new", it unconsciously tells others that you are rich. Furthermore, there is a widespread concern from sociologists that parents are sharing too much personal information on social-networking sites. All these unaware actions have probably contributed a lot more crimes.

4 In conclusion, it is impossible for us to stop the development of the advanced technology and there are benefits of these devices, but the disadvantages do outweigh the advantages. Before properly evaluating these devices, we should use it carefully. Otherwise, we will be regretting every now and then when something bad happens.

作文中譯加解析

/////////////

Unit 1
Unit 2
Unit 3
Unit 4
Unit 5
Unit 6
Unit 7
Unit 8
Unit 9
Unit 10
Unit 11
Unit 12
Unit 13
Unit 14
Unit 15

隨著許多科技裝置開發，我們曝露在危險的世界。有些人宣稱犯罪率將大幅地下降，如果我們有更多這些像是安全監視器的裝置。其他人認為這毫無幫助擔憂科技發展將導致比我們所能想像的到更嚴重的問題。你的看法是？

1 自從我們年少不更事的時代，科技進步已提供了我們生活上的舒適和便利，但是科技進步的進展也導致了幾個問題，其中一個與我們的生活最相關的是安全上的問題。

- 首段以單刀直入的方式，寫出題目所問的主題句，先引入主題，說明科技進步的好處，也提出科技進步的進展也導致了幾個問題，其中最與我們生活攸關的是我們的安全。

2 幾乎每個地方，從校園，公司大樓，每個街道，都有監控攝影機。從政府的觀點來說，設立的攝影機，能有效的減低犯罪致某個程度。而從市民的觀點來看，監控攝影機就像是安慰劑一樣，彷彿走在街上是安全的。即使有人闖空門，我們總是能由監控攝影機追蹤記錄且找到罪犯。但政府跟市民又是以什麼去保證監控攝影機的設立能大幅度地減低犯罪率。現實生活中如果人們意圖犯罪，他們還是會犯罪。他們將監控攝影機的方向移轉到其他方向，然後犯罪。他們並不在乎是否有監控攝影機。

- 第二段的說明從政府的觀點和多數市民的觀點開始，監控攝影機無所不在的存在價值。但也提出反問，及舉證質疑監控攝影機是否真的能有效地嚇阻犯罪。

3 而且還有其他考量因素，隨著其他裝置的開發，人們更曝露於易受監控的環境下。在缺乏謹慎的考量下，人們使用所謂的社群網站，其實是最易受到科技危害的。隨著私人資訊的被揭露，更易成為犯罪的受害者。例如於臉書上分享購買 BMW 新車，寫著 "剛入手" 或 "新的"，無意中告知其他人，你很富有。此外，社會學者也廣泛的關注有關父母在社群網站上分享太多個人資訊的問題。所有這一些不經意的動作已經有可能會因此造成許多犯罪。

- 此段接續上段的論點，提出另一種因為科技發展，人們在享受科技的便利性之餘還有可能會有各資外洩的狀況，以最流行的社群網站為例，也是成為引起犯罪的原因。

4 結論是我們不可能去阻止先進科技的發展，而這些裝置對我們來說也有益處的，但是弊大於利。在適當的評估這些裝置之前，我們都應謹慎地使用。否則，當壞事發生時，我們將不時感到後悔。

- 最後以 In conclusion 衍生法作為總結，結論中說明不可能因為這樣的原因就放棄科技的發展，反之是我們要謹慎的使用，並說明原因。

字彙補一補

1. trigger **v.** 引起

This has triggered another problem.

這引起了另一個問題。

2. villain **n.** 惡棍

The villain should be sent to the prison.

這個惡棍應該被送進監獄。

3. switch **v.** 轉換

Switching from right to left is not easy.

從右轉到左不容易。

4. so-called **adj.** 所謂的

This is so-called the sugar daddy.

這就是所謂的甜心爸爸。

5. widespread **adj.** 廣佈的

The drinkable problem is so widespread that people directly purchase water from other countries.

到處都有飲用水的問題，所以人們直接從其他國家購買水。

6. impossible **adj.** 不可能的

It is impossible for us to hire a person who has a large tattoo on his arm.

我們不可能雇用一個在手臂上有大幅刺青的人。

重點解析

1. But in what ways can governments and citizens guarantee the crime rate will be significantly reduced if security cameras are erected?

但政府跟市民又是以什麼去保證監控攝影機的設立能大幅度地減低犯罪率？

- if 表示如果…，引導副詞子句，其句型為 if+S+V，S+V(主要子句)，governments and citizens can guarantee the crime rate will be significantly reduced 為主要子句。
- be significantly reduced 為大幅減低。
- if security cameras are erected 表示如果監視器裝上了。

5. With their personal information being revealed, they are likely to be victims of the crime.

隨著私人資訊的被揭露，更易成為犯罪的受害者。

- with 為介系詞，表示然而。
- are likely to 表示可能，為常見片語。
- victims of the crime 表示犯罪的犧牲者。
- With their personal information being revealed 表示隨著個人資訊被揭露。

6. Furthermore, there is a widespread concern from sociologists that parents are sharing too much personal information on social-networking sites.

此外，社會學者也廣泛的關注有關父母在社群網站上過度分享個人資訊的問題。

- if…表示條件句引導一副詞子句，為 if+S+V 的句型。
- There is/there are 為常用的基本句型，其句型後常接代名詞或名詞，再加上時間或地點。
- a widespread concern 表示廣大的關注。
- are sharing too much 表示分享過多。

such... (thrive on) 這類的…（隨處可見）

可以這樣寫

//////////

1. Such voluminous plants thrived on ancient jungles.

   如此體態龐大的植物於遠古叢林中隨處可見。

2. Such muscular bodies thrive on the runway.

   如此健碩的身材在伸展台上隨處可見。

句型小貼士

- thrive 表示興旺/茂盛/繁榮，是常用字，其後常與介系詞 on 搭配，thrive on 有…隨處可見等意思。

- such 表示這類的/諸如此類的，若與 that 搭配有如此…以至於的意思，於考試中極為常見，也常用於表示加強語氣和表示驚嘆。

- 例句 1 與例句 2 僅差在 such 和 thrive on 後所加的敘述的不同，分別為 voluminous plants 搭 ancient jungles 和 muscular bodies 搭 the runway。

句型腦激盪

★Such giant plants thrived on ancient jungles.
⇨ Such giant plants with huge fruits thrived on ancient jungles.
具有這樣碩大果實的龐大植物於遠古叢林中隨處可見。

★Such animals thrived on ancient jungles.
⇨ Such animals with wings thrived on ancient jungles.
像這樣有羽翼的動物於遠古叢林中隨處可見。

★Such slim figures thrived on runway shows.
⇨ Such slim figures of models thrived on runway shows.
如此體態苗條的模特兒於展示台表演中隨處可見。

★Such students thrive on highly developed cities.
⇨ Such students with fantastic ideas thrive on highly developed cities.
有這類極佳想法的學生於高度發展的城市中隨處可見。

★Such housewives thrived on people of the previous generation.
⇨ Such housewives with great cooking skills thrived on people of the previous generation.
具如此良好廚藝技能的家庭主婦於上個世代中隨處可見。

★Such husbands thrive on civilized cities.
⇨ Such husbands with great communication skills thrive on civilized cities.
如此具良好溝通能力的丈夫於現代化都市中隨處可見。

★Such children thrive on modern cities.

⇨Such children with attention disorders thrive on modern cities.

像這樣有注意力問題的小孩於現代都市隨處可見。

★Such creatures thrived on ancient jungles.

⇨Such creatures with terrific hunting skills thrived on ancient jungles.

如此具極佳獵捕能力的生物於遠古叢林中隨處可見。

★Such habitat at all thrives on inland areas.

⇨Such habitat with no rainfall at all thrives on inland areas.

如此無降雨量的棲地於內陸地區隨處可見。

Instagram PO文小練習

Tips：such 後接名詞，thrive on 後面接可見到 such 後名詞的地點

Such _____ thrive(s/d) on _____

_____

作文範例

Students are now more willing to study abroad thanks to scholarship offered by overseas universities. They have the chance to experience a unique university life in other countries right after the high school ceremony. Parents are now more open to this, knowing that scholarships offered by those universities is able to cover four years of tuition fee and many other things. What is your opinion?

1 It is true that people tend to choose to study in their own country when it comes to pursue a higher learning, but with campus exhibitions and other orientation-related things from other nations being introduced, high school students have more choices. Parents are also more open to this simply because they want their kids to have a brighter future.

2 It is a cliché to say that studying abroad can broaden your horizons, but it is so true. Being in such an international setting is an invaluable experience. Furthermore, most excellent universities are now offering scholarships for students with potentials and high entrance exam records. Also, it is great for them to develop their independence, interpersonal skills, and many other things, which are vital for their career development. Some students are choosing to study abroad even if they can enter several top universities in Taiwan. The trend to this development is attributed to the low salary in recent years, and parents want their kids to be more competitive in the future.

3 Although studying abroad may package students with lots of professional attributes and learning experiences, some students seem to have a problem with it. Some are having problems adapting to new surroundings, while others are experiencing culture barriers. But no matter what, it won't affect those who might think that when the opportunity presents itself; it is a waste if you choose not to go.

4 To conclude, studying abroad is worthwhile. Every good thing has its downside. Keeping a positive mind is the key to all things. We should grab every opportunity whether it is finding a job or studying abroad. After all chances wait for no man.

作文中譯加解析

多虧了海外大學提供的獎學金，學生更有意願出國留學。他們有機會在高中畢業典禮結束後，在其他國家經歷獨特的大學生活。父母對這也更開放了，知道由這些大學提供的獎學金有包含四年的住宿費和許多事情。你的看法是？

1 當提到攻讀更高的學位時，人們的確傾向於在自己國家求學。但隨著校園展覽會和其他國家的新生介紹相關的事物的引進，高中生有了更多的選擇。父母也更為開放，因為他們希望自己的小孩有更光明的未來。

• 首段以 It is true…來引入主題，說明現狀，以及出國唸書盛行的原因。

2 出國唸書能拓展你的視野，儘管是陳腔濫調，但卻是真的。置身於如此的國際環境中是寶貴的經驗。此外，大多數卓越的大學現在都有提供給有潛力且入學考試成績高的學生獎學金。而且，出國唸書有助於培養獨立、人際關係技巧和許多能力，對於職涯發展是很棒的。有些學生即使能唸台灣幾所頂尖大學，卻選擇出國唸書。此發展的趨勢是因為近幾年的低薪趨勢所造成的，而父母更希望自己的小孩更具競爭力。

• 次段舉了幾種出國唸書的好處，以 cliché 來形容「出國唸書能拓展你的視野」的論調，但卻是不容忽視的事實。還提出因為近幾年的國內的低薪趨勢是造成父母送孩子出國讀書的原因。

63

3 儘管出國讀書能使學生具備更多的專業特質和學習經驗，但有些學生似乎有困難。有些是適應新環境的問題，而有些則是經歷文化隔閡。但是不管如何，這並不會影響到那一些認為這是千載難逢機會的學生，而選擇不去是浪費機會。

- 這一段舉出出國唸書可能會遇到的問題，但也說出許多人覺得出國唸書是值得把握的機會。以會遇上的問題，反向操作來支持自己的論點。

4 總而言之，出國唸書是值得的。每件好事都有其反面。關鍵在於對所有事都抱持正向的心態。我們需抓住每個機會，不論是找工作或者是求學。畢竟，機會是不等人的。

- 最後以 To conclude 做總結，延續第三段的反向操作，說明每件好的事都會有不好的地方，重要的是我們自己的心態，以抓住機會來支持自己的意見。

字彙補一補

1. brighter **adj.** 較光明的
   If you want to have a brighter future, you need to work hard.
   如果你想要前途較光明的未來，你需要努力。

2. international **adj.** 國際的
   International design schools are now offering scholarship.
   國際設計學校現在提供了獎學金。

3. excellent **adj.** 卓越的
   This hotel is known for its excellent service.
   這間旅館以卓越的服務聞名。

4. interpersonal **adj.** 人際關係的
   Interpersonal skills are important in the workplace.
   人際關係技巧在職場中是重要的。

5. competitive **adj.** 競爭的
   To be a competitive in the workplace, he participates in the training courses.
   為了要在職場中具競爭力，他參加了訓練課程。

6. worthwhile **adj.** 值得的
   Eventually, it proves that her courage of taking that step is quite worthwhile.
   最後證實她勇於採取那步是相當值得的。

重點解析

1. Furthermore, most excellent universities are now offering scholarships for students with potentials and high entrance exam records.

   此外，大多數卓越的大學現在都有提供給有潛力且入學考試成績高的學生獎學金。

   - furthermore 表示此外，為承轉詞。
   - are now offering scholarships 表示現在提供獎學金。
   - with potentials and high entrance exam records 表示具潛力和高的入學考試分數。

2. Also, it is great for them to develop their independence, inter-personal skills, and many other things, which are vital for their career development.

   而且，出國唸書有助於培養獨立、人際關係技巧和許多能力，對於職涯發展是很棒的。

   - also 表示此外，為承轉詞。
   - it is great for them 表示對他們來說是棒的…。
   - which 引導關係代名詞子句，句中為 which are vital for their career development 表示對他們的職涯發展是很重要的，which 修飾前面的 their independence, interpersonal skills, and many other things。

3. Although studying abroad may package students with lots of attributes and learning experiences, some students seem to have a problem with it.

儘管出國讀書能使學生具備更多的專業特質和學習經驗，但有些學生似乎有困難。

- although 在這裡表語氣轉折⋯，引導副詞子句，其句型為 Although+S+V，S+V（主要子句），some students seem to have a problem with it 為主要子句。
- package students with lots of attributes and learning experiences 表示使學生具備更多的特質和學習經驗，。
- seem to have a problem with it 表示有些學生似乎有困難。

if... conjure up..., S+V...
如果⋯想起/映入眼簾

可以這樣寫

1. If the photo conjures up memories of your ex, you'd better keep it in the closet.

   如果照片使你腦海中浮現出你前任的回憶，你最好將它置於櫃子裡。

2. If the scenery conjures up inspiration for the next painting project, you'd better write that down.

   如果景色使你腦海中浮現出下個繪畫計劃的靈感，你最好將它寫下。

句型小貼士

- If 的用法極為常見，if 所引導的子句為副詞子句，句型為 If 引導副詞子句，主要子句(S+V)⋯。

- conjure up 為使腦海中⋯浮現/使⋯映入眼簾的意思，亦有如魔術般變出的意思。

- had better 為最好⋯，注意其後加原形動詞。

68

[⚡] 句型腦激盪

★If the photo conjures up memories of your ex, you'd better keep it in the closet.

⇨If the photo that you've found in the red box conjures up memories of your ex, you'd better keep it in the closet.

如果你在紅色箱子裡找到的照片使你腦海中浮現出你前任的回憶，你最好將它置於櫃子裡。

★If the candies conjure up memories of your childhood, you can try to find them from some shops.

⇨If the candies with numerous colors conjure up memories of your childhood, you can try to find them from some shops.

如果不同顏色的糖果使你腦海中浮現出你童年的回憶，你可以試著從有些店裡找到它們。

★If the ingredients conjure up your class nutrition analysis report, it's time for you to relax.

⇨If the ingredients with nutritional values conjure up your class nutrition analysis report, it's time for you to relax.

如果具營養價值的成分使你腦海中浮現出你課堂營養分析報告，是表示你該好好放鬆了。

★If the performance conjures up memories of your stage performance, you'd better not to take it too serious.

⇨If the performance with special attention conjures up memories of your stage performance, you'd better not to take it too serious.

如果引人注目的表演使你腦海中浮現出你的舞台表現，你最好別將它看得太重。

★If the drug conjures up your unpleasant memories, you'd better try not to think about it.

⇨ If the appearance of the drug conjures up your unpleasant memories, you'd better try not to think about it.

如果藥品的外觀使你腦海中浮現出你不好的回憶，你最好試著不去想它。

★If the drink conjures up your trip to other countries, you'd better write it in your diary.

⇨ If the color of the drink conjures up your trip to other countries, you'd better write it in your diary.

如果飲品的顏色使你腦海中浮現出你到其它國家旅行，你最好將它寫入你的日記裡。

★If the music conjures up joyful memories, you can share it with your friends.

⇨ If the sound of the music conjures up joyful memories, you can share it with your friends.

如果音樂的聲音使你腦海中浮現出喜悅的回憶，你可以與朋友分享它。

★If the film conjures up software you just learned, you can utilize them immediately.

⇨ If the special effects of the film conjures up software you just learned, you can utilize them immediately.

如果電影的特效使你腦海中浮現出你剛學的軟體，你能立即利用他們。

★If the meal conjures up a feeling of worthiness, you don't have to hide your joyfulness.

⇨ If the discount of the meal conjures up a feeling of worthiness, you don't have to hide your joyfulness.

如果餐點的折扣使你腦海中浮現出值得的感覺，你不用隱藏你的喜悅。

★If the advertisement conjures up a feeling of unworthiness, it is time for you to consider finding other companies.

⇨If the cost of the advertisement conjures up a feeling of unworthiness, it is time for you to consider finding other companies.

如果廣告的花費使你腦海中浮現出不值得的感覺，是時候你該考慮其他公司了。

Instagram PO文小練習

Tips：要記住在 If 後面引導的是副詞子句，再接上主要子句(S+V)。

If _____ conjure(s) up_____

_____

作文範例

According to the Chinese tradition, people have a higher expectation toward people who are thirty. They are expected to be responsible for many things either in the workplace or in the family. It seems like they have plenty of choices, but they don't. They are expected to get married and have kids, but some females say they are not child-making machines. Others claim that staring a marriage is complicated, and they are not ready to be in the same room with their mother-in-law. What is your opinion?

1 When people turn to thirty years old, people have a certain expectation. It is also a moment for a person to become independent, according to eastern traditions, but getting married is not the case.

2 Not all people are suitable for getting married. Starting a marriage is more complicated than we think. People have all their right for getting married or not. For some, they are not quite ready for a marriage. For others, they have other options.

3 With more people choosing to study for their M.A. or PhD in other foreign countries, it stands to reason that they will not choose to get married in their twenties. It is way too soon for them to start a marriage. It is even more ridiculous that some people ask their parents to pay for the wedding fees and many other things. Other than those silly reasons, people tend to get married when they are prepared or at least have enough savings. You cannot possibly get married when you are in debt. Furthermore, no girls want to marry a guy who is still in debt for their tuition debts while earning their 22k salaries. Girls now have set extra high standards because getting married and having kids are not that easy.

4 Overall, it is true that getting married when you are thirty will benefit the society and you. But there is nothing wrong if you get married after thirty. Also, there is nothing wrong if you choose to be single as long as you are happy. We don't have to do something that is against our will just because you care about how other people feel. Getting married just because other people want you to or others were doing it will certainly loose the point of marriage.

作文中譯加解析

根據中國傳統，人們對於三十歲的人有更高的期望。他們被期待在家庭或職場上要負責更多事情。他們看似有許多選擇，但其實不然。他們被期待要結婚然後有小孩，但是許多女性說他們並不是生小孩機器。其他人說開啟一段婚姻是很複雜的，他們還沒準備好能與自己的婆婆待在同個房間裡。你的看法是？

1 當邁入 30 歲時，人們的確會有特定的期待。根據東方人的傳統，這個時期也是人變得更獨立的時候。但結婚卻不是。

- 首段以題目中所提到的在 30 歲前結婚的好處，提出以文化方面的看法，但最後一句表達自己的立場，表示不同意這樣的說法。

2 並非所有人都適合結婚。要開始一段婚姻遠比我們想像中還要更為複雜。人們有權選擇結婚還是不結婚。對某些人來說，他們尚未準備好步入婚姻。對其他人來說，他們有其他的選擇。

- 第二段說明自己的論點，以要開始一段婚姻的複雜性，人們選擇結婚與否的權力等來闡述。

3 隨著更多人選擇於其他國家攻讀碩士或博士，他們理所當然的不會在二十幾歲時就結婚。對他們來說此時結婚太早了。更令人感到荒謬的是由父母支付婚姻開銷和其他事物。除了那些愚蠢因素，人們傾向於準備好時或至少有足夠存款時再步入婚姻。人們不可能在負債時選擇結婚。再者,沒有女生會選擇嫁給一個仍有學貸且收入兩萬二的男生。現在的女生大多對此設定了高標準,因為結婚和有小孩都不是件容易的事。

- 這一段以現今的高學歷現象來輔助支持自己的論點,還有舉行婚禮及組織家庭所要付出的開支等舉證支持在 30 歲之前就結婚的困難度。

4 總括來說,在 30 歲前結婚對社會跟個人來說的確是有助益的。但是 30 歲後才結婚也沒什麼不對。而且選擇維持單身也沒什麼不對,只要你自己過的快樂就好。我們不必要做任何違背自己意願的事,只是因為你在意其他人怎麼看待。如果結婚只是為了別人想要你這樣做或是因為別人也都是這樣的話,就完全失去了婚姻的意義。

- 以 Overall 這一個總結語,來做結論。闡明文章中所寫的論點,對於在 30 歲之前結婚應該是因人而異,應該以個人意願為最主要的考量,並再次說明。

75

字彙補一補

1. independent **adj.** 獨立的
   Some tourists like independent trails.
   有些觀光客喜歡獨立的步道。

2. suitable **adj.** 合適的
   You are not suitable for this job.
   你不適合這份工作。

3. complicated **adj.** 複雜的
   It is complicated than we think.
   這比我們想像中更複雜。

4. foreign **adj.** 國外的
   Foreign languages are hard to learn.
   外語很難學習。

5. silly **adj.** 愚蠢的
   Asking a silly question is unacceptable.
   問愚蠢的問題是不能接受的。

6. possibly **adv.** 可能地
   You cannot possibly find a job in New York with a mediocre degree.
   你不可能以平庸的學歷在紐約找到工作。

重點解析

1. Starting a marriage is more complicated than we think.

   要開始一段婚姻遠比我們想像中還要更為複雜。

   - Starting a marriage…為動名詞當主詞其後加單數動詞。
   - Starting a marriage 表示展開一段婚姻。
   - more complicated than we think 表示比我們想得更複雜。

2. With more people choosing to study for their M.A. or PhD in other foreign countries, it stands to reason that they will not choose to get married in their twenties.

   隨著更多人選擇於其他國家攻讀碩士或博士，他們理所當然的不會在二十幾歲時就結婚。

   - with 為介系詞，With more people choosing to study for their M.A. or PhD in other foreign countries 表示隨著更多人選擇在國外攻讀他們的碩士和博士學歷。
   - it stands to reason that…表示…是理所當然的…。
   - will not choose to get married 不會選擇結婚。

3. Furthermore, no girls want to marry a guy who is still in debt for their tuition debts while earning their 22k salaries.

   再者，沒有女生會選擇嫁給一個仍有學貸且收入兩萬二的男生。

   - furthermore 表示此外…為承轉詞。
   - no 為否定詞，no girls…為沒有一個女孩。
   - who 引導關係代名詞子句，句中為 who is still in debt for their tuition debts 表示仍因為學貸而負債。

once (consid-ered..., S+V...)
曾經/一度被認為是…

 可以這樣寫 ///////////

1. Once considered hazardous, this plant has been proven to have some medication effects.

   一度被認為具危險性，此植物已被證實具有一些醫療效果。

2. Once considered a god send, this fish species has shown a high DDT concentration in the recent report.

   一度被認為是天賜之物，此魚種於近期報告中，已顯示出高量的 DDT 濃度。

句型小貼士 . . . .

- once 的用法極為常見，其用法也極廣泛，可以於句中當名詞/副詞/連接詞。

- has been proven 為現在完成被動式，句中表示已被證實具…。

- has shown 為現在完成式表示已顯示…。

⚡ 句型腦激盪

///////////

★Once considered a useful tool, this tool is actually outdated in many developed countries.

⇨Once considered an extremely useful tool, this tool is actually outdated in many developed countries.

一度被認為是有用的工具,此工具在許多已開發國家是過時的。

★Once considered a legend, this building has led to a crowd of people to visit.

⇨Once considered an urban legend, this building has led to a crowd of people to visit.

一度被認為是都市傳説,此建築物導致了許多人到訪。

★Once considered a legendary figure, the supermodel is deciding to retire.

⇨Once considered a legendary figure of this century, the supermodel is deciding to retire.

一度被認為是這個世紀的傳奇人物,此超模正決定退休。

★Once considered a well-known celebrity, the celebrity had several renowned performances on the stage.

⇨Once considered a well-known celebrity to every household, the celebrity had several renowned performances on the stage.

一度被認為是家喻戶曉的名人,這位名人有幾個知名的舞台表現。

★Once considered a harmful hazard, this hazard has now been proven that it is not harmful.

⇨Once considered a potentially harmful hazard, this hazard has now been proven that it is not harmful.

一度被認為是具潛在危害的危險物，此危險物已被證實是不具危害的。

★Once considered a gift, it is sad to know that it's a danger for our citizen.

⇨Once considered a great gift, it is sad to know that it's a danger for our citizen.

一度被認為極佳的禮物，很遺憾的知道這對我們市民是危險的。

★Once considered a mystery, it is revealed thanks to our technology.

⇨Once considered a little-known mystery, it is revealed thanks to our technology.

一度被認為是鮮為人知的謎團，多虧了我們的科技，謎團已揭露。

★Once considered a mythology, now there is evidence to back it up.

⇨Once considered an iconic mythology, now there is evidence to back it up.

一度被認為具象徵性的神話，現在有個證據去支持它。

★Once considered a rumor, the news, on the other hand, has confirmed that it is a lie.

⇨Once considered a destructive rumor, the news, on the other hand, has confirmed that it is a lie.

一度被認為具毀滅性謠傳，新聞證實了這其實是謊話。

★Once considered a lie, unfortunately, we've found that it's just an ad tactic.

⇨Once considered a white lie, unfortunately, we've found that it's just an ad tactic.

一度被認為是善意的謊言，很不幸地我們卻發現這只是個廣告手法。

Instagram PO文小練習

Tips：Once considered 後面接名詞，再加上為什麼不再如此的原因。

Once considered _____

_____

作文範例

We all have pressure in our life. Sometimes the pressure has led to our overspending problems. Some, after a long working day, spend money buying things they don't need. Others who do not have money problems still buy lots of things from various channels. Of course, we do not want to be a shopaholic. What do you think is the solution to this phenomenon?

1 We buy lots of stuffs in our life. We buy meals we eat. We buy tickets if we travel. We buy drinks if we are thirsty. We also buy an expensive dress because our ancestors say clothes make a man. But there are huge differences among things we buy. Some are required because it is essential for our living. Others are not necessary. We can simply live without it.

2 Occasionally, we can indeed be led into buying unnecessary items we cannot afford. For example, we certainly do not need an expensive car to live. It is just a way to show off. But even if people are aware of the line between things that are required and things that are unnecessary, they are still trapped into this scheme.

3 Our desire of wanting things aggravates the behavior. We use our credit card to buy a trendy iPhone 6 simply because other people are having it and showing the photo on the so-cial-networking site. The advertisement also tricks us into the illusion that we want it so bad and we have to own it. Therefore, we have the psychological urge to buy stuffs in a few seconds but regret for buying them moments later.

4 One way of dealing with this problem is to set a strict goal based on our monthly payment. We have to buy things based on our salary. Do not use credit cards and other simi-lar things. Paying in cash is always the best policy. Also, buy things that you truly need.

5 In a nutshell, once you are tricked into buying things, you are in a vicious cycle. You will not be tricked into buying un-necessary things if you have formed a good habit. You will be glad to know how much money could have been saved if you stay away from temptations.

作文中譯加解析

　　我們生活中總有壓力。有時候壓力已導致我們過度花費的問題。有些在一個長工作天後,將錢花於他們不需要的事情上。其他沒金錢問題的人仍從其他管道買了許多東西。當然我們不想成為購物狂。你覺得此現象的解決之道是如呢?

1 我們一生中購買很多東西。我們購買每餐所吃的食物。如果旅遊時,我們買票券。當我們口渴時,我們買喝的。我們還會買昂貴的服飾,因為我們的祖先說,人要衣裝。但以上我們所購買的東西是有很大的區別的,有些是必需的,對我們生活來說是很重要的。有些則是不必要的,我們可以維持生活,而不受其影響。

• 首段先引入主題,先說明一生中會購買很多東西。並也將購買的東西做分類,藉以引出主題–購買不需要的東西。

2 偶爾我們會被誤導購買了我們根本付不起的非必須用品。例如,我們根本不需要昂貴的汽車過活。這僅僅是炫耀的方式。但是,即使人們清楚地知道必需品和非必需品的界限,他們仍受到蒙蔽。

• 第二段承接上段的非必需品,並以昂貴的車子為例,並指出人們清楚地知道必需及非必需品的差別,但有時就會無法抑制自己的慾望。

3 我們想要某些物品的慾望,加重了此行為。我們以信用卡購買時髦的 iPhone 6,只因為其他人也擁有,而且將其照片放置在社群網站上。廣告誘使我們並製造出我們非常想要它，我們必須擁有它的假象。因此，心理上的衝動驅使我們在幾秒內購買了物品，但是於稍後卻感到後悔。

• 此段同樣承接了上一段的非必需品討論，並更進一步的談到了人的慾望以及廣告的誘惑。

4 解決此問題的方法就是根據每月的薪資設定嚴格目標。買東西都基於自己薪資。不使用信用卡和類似的東西，都以現金購物為上策。還有只購買有實際需求的物品。

• 根據上面幾段的論述來提出解決方法。以自己的薪資衡量，並以現金購物，不購買不需要的物品。

5 簡單的來說，一旦你受到誘惑，你會陷入惡性循環。如果養成良好的習慣，你就不會被誘使去購買不需要的東西。如果你遠離那些誘惑，當發現省了多少錢後，你將會喜出望外。

• In a nutshell–簡言之、簡單的説，在這裡當作本文的總結，有結合上面一些説法及論點而得出的結論之意。以解決方法（養成良好習慣）及好處（省下的錢）做為結論。

字彙補一補

1. thirsty **adj.** 口渴的

   If you are thirsty, you can buy the drinks from the peddler.

   如果你口渴，你可以從小販那買飲料。

2. expensive **adj.** 昂貴的

   This is quite expensive.

   這相當昂貴。

3. difference **n.** 差異、不同

   The difference relies not in the quality but in the quantity.

   差異不在品質而是數量。

4. unnecessary **adj.** 不需要的

   A hat is considered an unnecessary item when swimming.

   當游泳時，帽子被視為是不需要的項目。

5. advertisement **n.** 廣告

   Advertisement is everywhere.

   廣告到處都是。

6. illusion **n.** 錯覺、假象

   This has created an illusion for most fans.

   這已經對大多數的粉絲造成錯覺。

重點解析

1. Therefore, we have the psychological urge to buy stuffs in a few seconds and regret for buying them moments later.

   因此，心理上的衝動驅使我們在幾秒內購買了物品，而於稍後卻感到後悔。

   - **Therefore** 為因此，表因果。承接上一句的「廣告誘使我們…」（原因），而這一句為結果。
   - **the psychological urge** 表示心理衝動。
   - **buy stuffs in a few seconds** 表示幾秒內買東西。
   - **regret for buying them moments later** 表示幾分鐘之後就後悔購買。

2. One way of dealing with this problem is to set a strict goal based on our monthly payment.

   解決此問題的方法就是根據每月的薪資設定嚴格目標。買東西都基於自己的薪資。

   - **One… of…** 表「…之一」，其後加單數動詞。
   - **set a strict goal** 表示設定一個嚴格的目標。
   - **based on our monthly payment** 表示基於我們每月薪資。
   - **that** 引導關係代名詞子句，句中省略 **that is**，原句為 **that is based on our monthly payment**。

click the "Like" button
按/點讚‥‥‥‥

可以這樣寫

1. People who click the like button for friends' Facebook content are considered supportive.
   替朋友臉書內容按讚的人被視為是支持的。

2. The person who clicks the like button for lover's Facebook content is thought of as a considerate gesture.
   替情人臉書內容按讚的人被認為是很體貼的表示。

句型小貼士

- who 的用法極為常見，其引導關係代名詞子句，也為常考要點。

- People who…其主要動詞為 are 在後方，who 引導的子句補充說明 people。

- 例句 1 與例句 2 除了主詞不同外，僅差在搭配的片語的不同，例 1 使用 be considered+形容詞，而例 2 使用 be thought of as 加名詞片語 a considerate gesture。

[⚡] 句型腦激盪

///////////

★People who click the like button for lover are considered considerate.

⇨People who click the like button for lover's Facebook content are considered considerate.

替愛人臉書內容按讚的人被視為是體貼的。

★People who click the like button for the news are considered news lovers.

⇨People who click the like button for the just released news are considered news lovers.

替剛發佈的新聞按讚的人被視為是新聞愛好者。

★People who click the like button for the anecdote are considered a curious person.

⇨People who click the like button for the well-known anecdote are considered a curious person.

替知名趣聞按讚的人被視為是好奇的人。

★People who click the like button for the advertisement are considered a fan of certain brand.

⇨People who click the like button for the advertisement shown on the Facebook are considered a fan of certain brand.

替顯示在臉書廣告按讚的人被視為是特定品牌的迷。

★People who click the like button for public figures are considered politics lovers.

⇨People who click the like button for public figures with a frequent exposure are considered politics lovers.

替頻頻曝光的公眾人物按讚的人被視為是愛好政治的人。

89

★People who click the like button for books are considered book lovers.

⇨People who click the like button for recently-published books are considered book lovers.

替近期出版書按讚的人被視為是愛好書的人。

★People who click the like button for pictures of a new cell-phone are considered as not jealous person.

⇨People who click the like button for pictures of a new cell-phone which is gifted by a friend are considered as not jealous person.

替「朋友送的手機」這種照片按讚的人被視為是不忌妒的人。

★People who click the like button for photos with special effects are considered a visual person.

⇨People who click the like button for photos with special effects are considered a visual person.

替有特效相片按讚的人被視為是視覺系的人。

 Instagram PO文小練習

✧ Tips：是誰按了個「讚」？在你眼中，這是一個怎麼樣的人呢？People who 也可以替換成人名、或是不同人稱等。

People who click the like button for ＿＿

_____

作文範例

Advertising is everywhere, from the billboard on the office building to advertising contents on social networking sites. It's often said that we buy things we not necessarily need, and the power of advertising certainly triumphs our needs. What is your opinion?

1 Nowadays, with technological changes in media, Internet, and other social networking sites, it seems that lots of marketing strategies and advertising companies have found a gold mine from there. The use of marketing strategies through those platforms has created more business opportunities. The sale of popular consumer goods has also skyrocketed.

2 With all these marketing and advertising strategies rampant in those channels we frequently use, it really makes us wonder do the high sales of popular consumer goods reflect the power of advertising? Or do the high sales of popular consumer goods reflect genuine needs of consumers?

3 Those advertising messages have constantly brainwashed us and we often buy things more than we need. People without critical thinking are susceptible to advertising messages, buying one thing after another. Some people even buy things from the like buttons of Facebook contents clicked by their close friends. It stands to reason that people tend to buy things not based on the real needs of the individuals, but based on the power of advertising.

4 The effects of the advertising have tricked us into believing we have to keep up with the Jones. People want to have things other people have. For example, the launch of the advertising campaign of the smartphone has led to the phenomenon of people's craze about smartphone. The result will not do us any good. It is obvious that for most companies the produce of goods is all about having tremendous profits instead of benefiting the whole society.

5 To summarize, for all these above-mentioned reasons, there is no denying that those glamorous ad contents affect the way we behave. It's obvious that we need to develop our critical thinking ability to avoid being brainwashed when viewing those eye candy ad contents.

作文中譯加解析

　　廣告無處不在，從辦公大樓的廣告看板到社交網站上的廣告內容。據說我們通常買了我們不見得需要的東西，廣告的力量確實勝過我們的需求。你的看法是？

1 現今，隨著媒體，網路，和其他社交網站，似乎許多行銷策略和廣告公司從那裡找到了金礦。透過那些平台所使用的行銷策略已創造了更多商機。流行消費者商品也已如日長虹。

- 首段定義隨著社交網站的發展及那些平台所使用的行銷策略，所帶來的影響。

2 隨著所有這些行銷和廣告策略在許多我們常用的頻道蔓延開來，這使得我們思考著流行消費者商品是否真的反應出廣告的力量又或者是反應出消費者真實需求呢？

- 第二段說明隨著這些東西的使用並提問，使得我們思考著流行消費者商品是否真的反應出廣告的力量又或者是反應出消費者真實需求呢？

3 這些廣告訊息已不斷地對我們洗腦，而且我們通常買超過我們需求的東西。缺乏批判性思考的人更易受到廣告訊息影響，買完這個又買下一個。有些人甚至是因為親近友人點臉書訊息讚而做出購買行為。人們理所當然的傾向買了非基於本身需求的東西，而是基於廣告的力量。

- 第三段定義這些廣告訊息已不斷地對我們洗腦，並指出缺乏批判性思考的人更易受到廣告訊息影響，人們理所當然的傾向買了非基於本身需求的東西，而是基於廣告的力量。

4 廣告的影響誘使我們思考著我們需要跟上別人的腳步。人們想要許多其他人也有的東西。例如，智慧型手機的廣告活動已導致人們對智慧型手機瘋狂的現象。這個結果並不會對我們有任何助益。很明顯對許多公司來說，商品的產生全是與巨額的利益有關而非使整個社會獲益。

- 第四段說明廣告的影響誘使我們思考著我們需要跟上別人的腳步。最後更指出很明顯對許多公司來說，商品的產生全是與巨額的利益有關而非使整個社會獲益。

5 總之，基於以上這些理由，無可否認的是，那些魅力的廣告內容影響我們行為表現的方式。顯而易見的是，我們需要發展我們的批判性思考能力，以免於在觀看那些賞心悅目的廣告內容時受到洗腦。

- 最後總結出流行消費者商品的高額銷售反應出廣告的力量而非反應出個人的真實需求。

字彙補一補

1. technological **adj.** 科技的
   This is certainly a technological advance.
   這確實是個科技進步。

2. skyrocket **v.** 暴漲
   The rice price has skyrocketed as a result of the shortage of rainfall these days.
   由於這些日子雨量的短缺，米價已暴漲。

3. popular **adj.** 流行的
   This popular song has comforted lots of people.
   這首流行歌撫慰了大多數的人。

4. susceptible **adj.** 易受攻擊的
   People who walk on the street after midnight are susceptible to be attacked.
   在午夜之後，走在街上的人是易受到攻擊的。

5. individual **n.** 個人
   People tend to buy things that are not on the basis of needs of the individuals.
   人們傾向買那些非基於個人需求的東西。

6. craze **n.** 狂熱
   People's craze for Harry Potter is well-known.
   人們對於哈利波特的狂熱是眾所皆知的。

重點解析

1. With all these marketing and advertising strategies rampant in those channels we frequently use, it really makes us wonder do the high sales of popular consumer goods reflect the power of advertising?

隨著所有這些行銷和廣告策略在許多我們常用的頻道蔓延開來,這使得我們思考著流行消費者商品是否真的反應出廣告的力量又或者是反應出消費者真實需求呢?

- with 表示隨著…,with all these marketing and advertising strategies rampant in those channels 表示隨著所有這些行銷和廣告策略在許多我們常用的頻道蔓延開來,those channels 後省略 that,其中 that 為受詞。
- it really makes us 表示…真的使我們…。
- do the high sales of popular consumer goods reflect the power of advertising「流行消費者商品是否真的反應出廣告的力量又或者是反應出消費者真實需求呢」,在句中為提問。

2. People without critical thinking are susceptible to advertising messages, buying one thing after another.

缺乏批判性思考的人更易受到廣告訊息影響,買完這個又買下一個。

- without 表示沒有…,其為介詞故其後加 N/Ving。
- are susceptible to 為常用的片語,表示易受…影響或易受…攻擊。
- buying one thing after another 表示買了一個又一個。

3. It is obvious that for most companies the produce of goods is all about having tremendous profits instead of benefiting the whole society.

很明顯對許多公司來説，商品的產生全是與巨額的利益有關而非使整個社會獲益。

- it is obvious…表示顯然是…。
- for most companies 表示對大多數的公司來説。
- instead of 表示而不是…，其後加 N/Ving。
- benefit the whole society 表示使整個社會受益。

 可以這樣寫

///////////

1. To be a well-known photographer, it means that besides talent and diligence, you also need some good luck.

　　要成為一位知名的攝影師，這表示除了天分及勤奮之外，你還需要一些好運。

2. To keep up with the Jones is the harmful trait that erodes one's humanity.

　　欲在物質等方面要趕上周遭的人是腐蝕著人性的有害的特質。

句型小貼士

- to+V 為不定詞其用法極為常見，也為常考要點，於句中為不定詞當主詞，其後主要動詞為單數。

- keep up with the Jones 指在物質等方面要趕上周遭的人，排場等要贏過親朋好友。

- 例句 1 後加 means to…表示前述部分是欲達成後面的目的，例句 2 為動詞後加名詞片語，其後加上關係代名詞補充說明 the harmful trait。

[⚡] 句型腦激盪

Unit 1
Unit 2
Unit 3
Unit 4
Unit 5
Unit 6
Unit 7
Unit 8
Unit 9
Unit 10
Unit 11
Unit 12
Unit 13
Unit 14
Unit 15

★To keep up with the current trend is not easy.

⇨ To keep up with the current trend is not as easy as tearing up a piece of paper.

要趕上當前趨勢是不容易的。

★To satisfy your girlfriend's vanity requires a sacrifice.

⇨ To satisfy your girlfriend's vanity requires a tremendous sacrifice.

要滿足你女朋友的虛榮心需要極大的犧牲。

★To stay positive in the workplace is not difficult.

⇨ To stay positive in the workplace is not that difficult.

在職場中保持正向並不那麼困難。

★To win over one's heart requires gifts.

⇨ To win over one's heart requires a lot of gifts.

要贏得某人歡心需要許多禮物。

★To avoid eating adulterated foods is not easy.

⇨ To avoid eating adulterated foods in our common life is not easy.

要避免在日常生活中吃到黑心食物是不容易的。

★To communicate with a boss requires a lot of patience.

⇨ To communicate with a stubborn boss requires a lot of patience.

要與固執的老闆溝通需要很有耐心。

★To find the prey in the desert sometimes requires luck.

⇨ To find the prey in the heated desert sometimes requires luck.

要在炎熱的沙漠中找到獵物有時候需要運氣。

★To find foods in the Arctic requires skills.

⇨ To find foods in the Arctic requires a lot of great skills.

在北極找尋食物需要許多高超的技巧。

★To watch a decent movie is hard.

⇨ To watch a decent movie in a rural town is hard.

要在鄉村小鎮看到像樣的電影是困難的。

★To convince your client to buy those products is slim.

⇨ To convince your client to buy those extremely expensive products is slim.

要說服你的客戶去買那些超貴的產品是微乎其微的。

Instagram PO文小練習

Tips：要做什麼事呢？要注意 To 後面接的是原形動詞！

To _____

_____

作文範例

Comments made by bosses and executives about recent graduates that they are unable to perform certain tasks have led us to think should universities only provide the knowledge rather than skills needed for the workplace? Aren't they responsible for graduates' job finding? What is your opinion?

1 Whether universities should provide students with access to knowledge for its own sake has long been debated. In real life, it really matters from subjects to subjects.

2 Although some subjects might seem not quite useful in school settings, they are fundamental to students' learning. Students may gradually develop their thinking abilities and habitually use those throughout the rest of their lives. Some subjects are emphasized on character formation and inter-personal skills.

3 Statements made by most bosses and executives about the newly-recruited graduates are somehow biased. Furthermore, a lot of works do not have adequate trainings. They only expect recently hired employees to be instantly used. But how can you expect newly-recruited graduates be in a completely new surrounding and is able to do jobs that require at least six months' training. Also, shifting all the blames to the schools is not only wrong, but also not helpful.

4 Employers have to provide newly-recruited employees with adequate trainings, but in reality to find a company that <u>provides employees with</u> adequate trainings is not easy. Moreover, it is the attitude that will ultimately be the determining factor for those graduates to be able to perform certain functions in the workplace. Also, companies should be more open and tolerant to graduates who are willing to learn and who have the right mindset. What they have learned during the past four years does not really matter. Motivation and passion are two keys that will get you there, while abilities are not.

5 From the above-mentioned statements, universities should provide students with access to knowledge, and assist students to develop the right mindset so that they are fully-prepared for job-finding and working.

作文中譯加解析

////////////

　　老闆和主管所陳述關於近期畢業生無法執行特定任務的評論，使得我們思考著大學應該只提供知識而非職場上所需要的技能嗎？他們難道對畢業生找工作不用負起任何責任嗎？你的看法是？

1 大學是否應該提供學生知識本身的汲取一直備受爭論。在現實生活中，這真的會因學科的不同而有所差異。

- 首段先定義大學是否應該提供學生知識本身的汲取一直備受爭論。

2 儘管有些學科在課堂環境下可能似乎不是相當的有用，但他們卻對學生的學習有根本的影響。學生可能逐漸發展出他們的思考能力，而終其一生習慣性的思考那些。而有些學科則強調人格養成和人際關係。

- 第二段指出有些學科在課堂環境下可能似乎不是相當的有用，但他們確對學生的學習有根本的影響。並說明有些學科是思考能力養成或強調人格養成和人際關係有關。

3 大多數老闆和主管對於近期雇用的畢業生的陳述是不公平的。此外，很多工作沒有適當的訓練。他們只期待近期雇用的員工能立刻上手。但你如何能夠期待剛雇用的畢業生在一個全新的環境中，且能夠上手那些需要六個月訓練的工作呢？而且，把責任都怪到學校不只是錯誤的，也毫無任何助益。

- 第三段指出大多數老闆和主管對於近期雇用的畢業生的陳述是不公平的。並提出反問你如何能夠期待剛雇用的畢業生在一個全新的環境中，且能夠上手那些需要六個月訓練的工作呢？

4 雇主必須提供新雇用的員工適當的訓練。但是在現實生活中要找到有提供員工訓練的公司不容易。此外，態度才是最終影響那些畢業生能否執行職場中某些工作的決定性因素。而且，公司應該更開放且對於願意學習且有正確心態的畢業生更容忍。他們四年所學的東西其實不重要。動力跟熱情是你能達到哪裡的兩個關鍵，而其他能力則不是。

- 第四段說明雇主必須提供新雇用的員工適當的訓練。並指出態度才是最終影響那些畢業生能否執行職場中某些工作的決定性因素。最後說明動力跟熱情是兩個關鍵。

5 總之，從以上的陳述中，大學應該提供學生知識的汲取，而且協助學生培養正確的心態所以他們才能在找工作跟工作時全然的準備好。

- 最後總結大學應該提供學生知識的汲取，而且協助學生培養正確的心態所以他們才能在找工作跟工作時全然的準備好。

字彙補一補

1. newly-recruited **adj.** 新雇用的
Executives are more tolerant of newly-recruited employees.
主管對於新雇用的員工更具容忍力。

2. completely **adv.** 完全地
This is completely different.
這是全然不同的。

3. shift **v.** 轉移
We are shifting from adding certain ingredients to adding new formula.
我們正從增加特定的成份轉移到增加新的配方。

4. employer **v.** 雇主
Employers are fear of hiring the person without any passion.
雇主害怕雇用到任何毫無熱情的人。

5. adequate **adj.** 適當的
An adequate amount of vitamin C is necessary.
有足夠的維生素 C 是必須的。

6. function **n.** 功能
The function of rainforest is like our lungs.
熱帶雨林的功能就像我們的肺。

重點解析

1. Although some subjects might seem not quite useful in school settings, they are fundamental to students' learning.

儘管有些學科在課堂環境下可能似乎不是相當的有用,但他們的確對學生的學習有根本的影響。

- although 表語氣轉折,引導副詞子句,其句型為 Although+S+V,S+V(主要子句),they are fundamental to students' learning 為主要子句。
- seem 表示似乎其後加形容詞。
- not quite useful 表示沒有相當實用。

2. But how can you expect newly-recruited graduates be in a completely new surrounding and is able to do jobs that require at least six months' training.

但你如何能夠期待剛雇用的畢業生在一個全新的環境中,且能夠上手那些需要六個月訓練的工作呢?

- newly-recruited graduates 表示新雇用的畢業生。
- a completely new surrounding 表示一個全新的環境。
- is able to 為常見片語表示能夠,其後加 V,另一常見片語為 be capable of。
- that 引導關係代名詞子句,句中為 that require at least 6 months' training 表示至少需要 6 個月的訓練。

3. Also, companies should be more open and tolerant to graduates who are willing to learn and who have the right mindset.

而且，公司應該更開放且對於願意學習且有正確心態的畢業生更容忍。

- also 表示而且。
- be more open 表示更開放，be tolerant to 表示容忍…。
- who 引導關係代名詞子句，句中為 who are willing to learn and who have the right mindset.，表示願意學習且有正確心態的，修飾 graduates 畢業生，and 為對等連接詞連接 who are willing to learn 和 who have the right mindset。

shy away from sth/sb...
避開/迴避

 可以這樣寫

/////////

1. Her goal is to shy away from the P.E. class.
   她的目標是避開體育課。

2. I've always shied away from speaking in public.
   我總是避免在公開場合發言。

句型小貼士

- 例句一為 to+V 的用法，在句中為不定詞用法。

- shy away from sth/sb 指因為緊張/擔心等因素而想避開某事或是某人。

- 例句 1 和例句 2 的主要差異為 from 後欲逃避的項目不同，一個是 the P.E. class，而另一個是 speaking in public。

⚡ 句型腦激盪

★She tries to shy away from the P.E. class.

⇨ She tries to shy away from the annoying P.E. class.
她試著避開惱人的體育課。

★The drug dealer shied away from the police.

⇨ The drug dealer shied away from the police on the street.
毒販避開街上的警方。

★Her intention is to shy away from the exercise.

⇨ Her intention is to shy away from the weekly exercise.
她的目的是避開每週運動。

★John's goal is to shy away from performing.

⇨ John's goal is to shy away from performing in the public.
John 的目的是要避開在公眾表演。

★Her goal is to shy away from speaking.

⇨ Her goal is to shy away from speaking in the auditorium.
她的目標是避開在講堂裡演說。

★He is trying to shy away from the snake.

⇨ He is trying to shy away from touching the snake.
他正試著避開觸摸蛇。

★She shies away from a guy that has a bad breath.

⇨ She shies away from second dating with a guy that has a bad breath.
她避免與有口臭的人約會第二次。

★Her purpose is to shy away from this interview.

⇨Her purpose is to shy away from this interview with her ex-boyfriend.

她的目的是避開這一次跟她前男友的面試。

★She likes to shy away from being alone.

⇨She likes to shy away from being alone in the empty apartment.

她喜歡避開單獨待在空的公寓裡。

★Her goal is to shy away from swimming in rivers.

⇨Her goal is to shy away from swimming in rivers with strong torrents.

她的目標是避開在具強激流的河裡游泳。

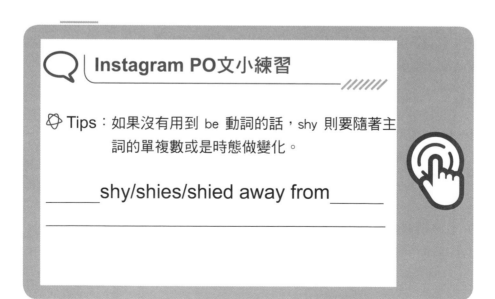

Instagram PO文小練習

Tips：如果沒有用到 be 動詞的話，shy 則要隨著主
詞的單複數或是時態做變化。

_____shy/shies/shied away from_____
_____

作文範例

Lots of factors affect people's job satisfaction. People rank particular factors on the list of the job satisfaction survey. Is it really that difficult for us to reach out satisfaction in the workplace? What is your idea?

1 Since the vast majority of people spend their time at work, at least a minimum of 8 hours per working day, the satisfaction of job is an important factor for people to remain at a company.

2 Job satisfaction is related to many areas, ranging from salaries, job content, relevance of one's expertise, colleagues, executives, and so on. Colleagues, for example, are people you have to work with all day long. If you cannot get along with your colleagues, it is highly unlikely for you to adapt to a new environment, let along working there for a long time or having great job satisfaction.

3 Furthermore, relevance of your expertise is also the key factor contributing to job satisfaction. A lack of certain or relevant expertise can have a great influence on how you are able to work there. A person is likely to be successful if he or she has relevant expertise. Also, even if people are willing to learn, they encounter more obstacles and are less competitive compared with people who are equipped with relevant experience and expertise.

4 To sum up, all the above mentioned factors have affected well-being of individuals in the workplace. People tend to have a different opinion on what is important and what is not. Some value certain factors more. Others rank particular factors on the list of the job satisfaction survey. It is highly unlikely for us to shy away from this topic, and say it is difficult for us to say that all people are satisfied with their work.

作文中譯加解析

　　許多因素影響著人們的工作滿意度。人們將某些特定的因素列於工作滿意度的調查上。而對我們而言要在職場上達到工作滿意度是真的有這麼困難嗎？你的看法是？

1 既然大多數的人花費他們的時間在工作，至少每個工作日八小時，工作的滿意度對人們來說是待在公司的重要因素。

- 首段先定義大多數的人花費他們的時間在工作，至少每個工作日八小時，工作的滿意度對人們來說是待在公司的重要因素。

2 工作滿意度與許多領域相關，從薪水，工作內容，每個人專長的相關性，同事，主管等等。例如同事是你每天必須相處的人。如果你沒辦法與同事相處，你也極不可能去適應一個新環境，更別說在那裡長時間工作了，或有多大的工作滿意度。

- 第二段說明工作滿意度與許多因素有關，而與同事相處影響由甚，更影響著你待在一家公司的時間長短。

3 此外，你專長的相關性也是促成你工作滿意度的關鍵因素。缺乏特定或相關的專長可能在你如何能在那裡工作有很大的影響。一個人能否成功端視他或她有相關的專長。而且，與具備相關經驗或專長的人相比之下，即使人們有意願學習，他們面臨更多障礙且較不具競爭力。

- 第三段定義專長的相關性也是促成你工作滿意度的關鍵因素。畢

竟，一個人能否成功端視他或她有相關的專長。即使人們有意願
學習，也比具備相關經驗或專長的人面臨更多的挑戰。

4 總之，所有上述提到的因素已經影響到個人於職場中的幸福感。人
們對於哪些重要而哪些不重要，傾向有不同的意見。有些人更重視
特定因素。其他人則把特定因素列於工作滿意度調查中。我們即不
可能閃避這個話題，而對我們來說所有人都對工作感到滿意是困難
的。

• 最後總結出這些因素已經影響到個人於職場中的幸福感。

字彙補一補

1. important **adj.** 重要的
It is important for us to be optimistic.
樂觀對我們來說是重要的。

2. remain **v.** 維持
She remains silent.
她保持緘默。

3. expertise **n.** 才能
Expertise refers to specific skills in certain areas.
專門技術指的是特定領域裡特別的技能。

4. competitive **adj.** 競爭的
Species have to stay competitive to survive.
物種必須維持競爭力才能生存。

5. equip **v.** 配有
Our lab is equipped with so much advanced equipment.
我們實驗室配有許多先進的設備。

6. tend **v.** 傾向
We tend to like the person who has a similar interest.
我們傾向喜歡有相似興趣的人。

重點解析

1. Job satisfaction is related to many areas, ranging from salaries, job content, relevance of one's expertise, colleagues, executives, and so on.

工作滿意度與許多領域相關，從薪水，工作內容，每個人專長的相關性，同事，主管等等。

> • be related to 表示與⋯相關。
> • range from A to B 表示從 A 到 B。
> • and so on 表示等等⋯。

2. A lack of certain or relevant expertise can have a great influence on how you are able to work there.

缺乏特定或相關的專長可能在你如何能在那裡工作有很大的影響。

> • a lack of 表示缺乏⋯。
> • have a great influence on 表示⋯對⋯有影響，需注意介系詞用 on。
> • are able to 表示能夠⋯。
> • how you are able to work there 表示你如何能在那裡工作。

3. Also, even if people are willing to learn, they encounter more obstacles and are less competitive compared with people who are equipped with relevant experience and expertise.

而且，與具備相關經驗或專長的人相比之下，即使人們有意願學習，他們面臨更多障礙且較不具競爭力。

- even if 表示即使，為語氣轉折…，引導副詞子句，其句型為 Even if+S+V，S+V(主要子句)。
- are willing to 表示願意…。
- encounter more obstacles and are less competitive 表示遭遇更多障礙和較少競爭力。其中 and 為對等連接詞連接 encounter more obstacles 和 are less competitive。
- compared with 表示對比，為與…相較之下。
- who 引導關係代名詞子句，句中為 who are equipped with relevant experience and expertise.表示配有相關經驗和技能。

Unit 12

even though
即使…

可以這樣寫

1. He has to guts to pursue Jane Even though he knows he is far out of her league.

   他有膽量追求珍，儘管他自知自己遠配不上對方。

2. Even though he is out of your league, you can still court him.

   即使知道配不上對方，妳仍可以追求他。

句型小貼士

- Even though 表示即使其用法極為常見，也為常考要點，其為從屬連接詞引導副詞子句。

- out of one's league 字面上指在某人的聯盟之外，其引申意思為超過某人的理解或能力範圍，或是某人高不可攀/配不上對方，意謂雙方條件落差太大追不到對方。

- have the guts 為口語常見用法，指有這個膽量或勇氣。

- 例句 1 和例句 2 的主要差異為敘述的部分不同，例句 1 多了片語 have the guts 的搭配。

[⚡] 句型腦激盪

★Even though the girl is friendly, she shouted at her father once.

⇨Even though the girl next door is friendly, she shouted at her father once.

即使鄰家女孩很友善，她曾吆喝她父親。

★Even though the boy is not handsome, he is very approachable.

⇨Even though the boy who's riding a bicycle is not handsome, he is very approachable.

即使騎著腳踏車的那個男孩不英俊，他非常平易近人。

★Even though our neighbors are easygoing, they have a dark secret.

⇨Even though our charming neighbors are easygoing, they have a dark secret.

即使我們的魅力鄰居很隨和，但他們有不可告人的秘密。

★Even though that boy is short, he is still very optimistic.

⇨Even though that boy who's the son of my friend is short, he is still very optimistic.

即使那個是我朋友兒子的男孩很矮，他仍非常樂觀。

★Even though the friend is not friendly, I still think of him as a friend.

⇨Even though the friend I met during the summer camp is not friendly, I still think of him as a friend.

即使這一個我在夏令營認識的朋友並不友善，我仍把他視為是朋友。

★Even though the reporter is married, she still has lots of fans.

⇨Even though the beautiful reporter is married, she still has lots of fans.

即使美麗的記者結婚了，她仍有許多粉絲。

★Even though the millionaire with a big heart, he is still misunderstood by people.

⇨Even though the millionaire with a big heart, he is still misunderstood by a lot of people.

即使百萬富翁寬宏大量，他仍被許多人誤解。

★Even though the man is not rich, he has lots of confidence that he will succeed.

⇨Even though the man from a lower rank is not rich, he has lots of confidence that he will succeed.

即使這個從較低階層的男人不富有，他有極大的自信他將會成功。

Q Instagram PO文小練習

Tips：Even though 後面要引導的為副詞子句。

Even though _____

_____

作文範例

It is true that people with an inborn ability certainly outweigh people who do not. But is it true that through training and learning, a lot of things can be gradually made up for? What is your opinion?

1 <u>Even though</u> our hereditary traits already determine who we are when we are born, teaching still has a great influence on our ability to become a good sports person or musicians.

2 It is true that people with an inborn ability certainly outweigh people who do not. But if people with great abilities are not utilizing their talents, it is a waste for them. In today's world, everything is possible as long as you are willing to learn. Furthermore, a lot of people have demonstrated their lack of abilities in several learning fields, but they have become successful players in their thirties and forties.

3 It seems that great talents will play a much bigger role in a person's success, but exhibit a slight influence on a person's late years. Moreover, through training and learning, a lot of things can be gradually made up for. A person who lacks muscle strength to be an athlete may get an extra help to achieve the goal as long as he sticks to it. Also, people who lack natural talents are humble. They are aware of their weaknesses. They know they have to work hard to catch up with others. This is also why a short person has to work extra hard to win the heart of someone and why a short person has a greater resistance to outer pressure than a tall person, according to a study.

4 To sum up, even though our genetic traits already determine who we are when we are born, teaching and willingness to learn still have a great influence on our ability to become a good sports person or musicians. We can still be those people through learning.

作文中譯加解析

////////////

　　的確，有天賦的人確實勝過不具天賦的人。但是透過訓練和學習，許多事情真的能有所補強嗎?你的看法是？

1 即使我們的遺傳特質已經於我們出生時決定了，教學仍對於我們是否能成為運動員或音樂家的能力有很大的影響。

- 首段說明遺傳特質已經於我們出生時決定了，但教學仍扮演極大的影響力。

2 具有與生俱來能力的人確實勝過不具天賦的人。但是如果具有人才能的人沒利用他們的天賦，對他們來說則是浪費。在現今世界，每件事都是可能的，只要你願意學習。此外，很多人都已經展現出他們在幾個學習領域上缺乏的特質，但是他們在 30 幾歲和 40 幾歲成了成功的運動員。

- 第二段說明俱有與生俱來能力的人確實勝過不具天賦的人。但也指出學習意願也扮演重要角色。並以其他人為例，說明肯學的態度使很多人最終得到成功的果實。

3 似乎巨大的才能會在每個人成功上扮演較大程度的角色，但是卻在個人晚年時卻顯示較輕微的影響。此外，透過訓練和學習很多事情是能逐漸補足的。一個人若欠缺肌肉強度而無法成為運動員，可能可以藉由額外的幫助達到目標，只要他堅持下去。而且，缺乏天賦的人很謙虛。他們意識到他們的缺點。他們知道他們需要努力以趕上其他人。這也是為什麼矮的人需要更額外的努力以贏得每個人的心，也是為什麼矮的人對外界壓力時所能程受的阻力遠高於身高高的人，這是根據一項研究指出。

- 第三段定義似乎巨大的才能會在每個人成功上扮演較大程度的角色，但是卻在個人晚年時卻顯示較輕微的影響。並舉例出由訓練能補足先天上的不足。另外也由身高的研究證明缺乏先天條件的人反而能受益。

4 總之，即使我們的遺傳特質已於我們出生時決定我們是誰，教學和願意學習仍對於我們成為運動員或音樂家有很大的影響。我們仍可能透過學習成為那些人。

- 最後總結出我們仍可能因為教學和願意學習讓我們成為運動員或音樂家。

字彙補一補

1. inborn **adj.** 天生的
   He does have an inborn talent in the basketball field.
   他在籃球領域確實有天賦。

2. gradually **adv.** 逐漸地
   The government is gradually adopting the approach.
   政府正逐漸採用這個方法。

3. extra **adj.** 額外的
   If you need an extra help, please let us know.
   如果你需要額外幫助，請讓我們知道。

4. achieve **v.** 達到
   It is important for us to achieve some personal goals.
   對我們來說達到有些個人目標是重要的。

5. resistance **n.** 阻力
   Resistance to move is the reason why she is having a fight with her husband.
   不願意搬家是她為什麼與她老公吵架的原因。

6. willingness **n.** 願意
   Willingness to learn is an important factor for you to succeed.
   願意學習對你成功是重要的因素。

🎥 重點解析

1. Furthermore, a lot of people have demonstrated their lack of abilities in several learning fields, but they have become successful players in their thirties and forties.

   此外，很多人都已經展現出他們在幾個學習領域上缺乏的特質，但是他們在 30 幾歲和 40 幾歲成了成功的運動員。

   - Furthermore 表示此外…為承轉詞。
   - But 為對等連接詞表示語氣轉折。
   - Have demonstrated 表示已展現出…。
   - In their thirties and forties 表示在他們三十和四十歲時。

2. It seems that great talents will play a much bigger role in a person's success, but exhibit a slight influence on a person's late years.

   似乎巨大的才能會在每個人成功上扮演較大程度的角色，但是卻在個人晚年時卻顯示較輕微的影響。

   - It seems that 表示似乎…。
   - Much 形容 bigger。
   - Play…role 表示扮演…角色。
   - But 為對等連接詞。
   - exhibit a slight influence on a person's late years 表示在個人晚年時卻顯示較輕微的影響。

3. A person who lacks muscle strength to be an athlete may get an extra help to achieve the goal as long as he sticks to it.

一個人若欠缺肌肉強度而無法成為運動員，可能可以藉由額外的幫助達到目標，只要他堅持下去。

- who 引導關係代名詞子句，句中為 who lacks muscle strength 表示缺乏肌力。
- may get an extra help 表示可能得到額外的幫助。
- to achieve the goal 表示達到目標。
- as long as 表示只要…。
- sticks to 表示堅持…。

 可以這樣寫

1. We should get started before the hotshot takes it.

   在高手下手之前，我們應該要先開始行動。

2. Grab anything you see at the department store before they sold out.

   在賣光之前，將任何你在百貨公司裡看到的東西都拿走。

句型小貼士

- before 表示即使其用法極為常見，也為常考要點，其為表時間的從屬連接詞引導副詞子句。

- hotshot 字面上指快手，其引申意思為藝高人膽大且有能力或具自信的人。

- grab anything you see 指拿任何你所見之物。

⚡ 句型腦激盪

★We should stop her before the girl gets in the train.

⇨We should stop her before the girl in the green suit gets in the train.

在穿綠色衣服的女孩上火車之前，我們該阻止她。

★We should tell the security before the boy parks his car.

⇨We should tell the security before the boy in the blue jacket parks his car.

在身穿藍色夾克的男孩將車停在這裡之前，我們該告訴保全。

★We should hang out with them more before our neighbors move out of the lane.

⇨We should hang out with them more before our charming neighbors move out of the lane.

在迷人的鄰居搬離巷子之前，我們該多跟他們聚聚。

★We should ask those girls out before other handsome guys move in to the dormitory.

⇨We should ask those girls out before other guys move in to the dormitory.

在其他英俊男士搬進宿舍之前，我們該邀那些女孩出去。

★We should do something before our competitors.

⇨We should do something before our competitors who are ruthless trick us.

在我們的競爭者無情地誘騙我們之前，我們該做些事。

★We should inform the boss before the teammate does.

⇨We should inform the boss before the teammate who wants to take it himself.

在同隊隊友想要把這個功勞歸功於他之前，我們該告知老闆。

★We should leave before that classmate says anything to you.

⇨We should leave before that classmate who is competitive says anything to you.

在那一個好勝的同學對你說任何話之前，我們該離開了。

★We should move to another platform before strangers come closer.

⇨We should move to another platform before strangers with an odd intention come closer.

在具奇怪意圖的陌生人更靠近之前，我們該移往另一個月台。

★We should get started before the cops start to look into the case.

⇨We should get started before the cops with aggressiveness start to look into the case.

在具進取心的警方開始查案之前，我們該動身了。

★You should finish your beef noodles before Johnny comes home.

⇨You should finish your beef noodles before Johnny who's a beef lover comes home.

Johnny 喜歡吃牛肉，在他到家前，你應該吃光你的牛肉麵。

Instagram PO文小練習

🔖 Tips：before 是表時間的從屬連接詞，用以表示在
什麼時間之前，如果要表示在什麼（位置）
前，則應該用 in front of。

_____before_____

_____

作文範例

It's often said that temptations are the greatest enemy, but shifting all the blames to the food does not help at all. People even make ridiculous claims of not being responsible for their weight. What is your opinion?

1 Temptations are the great obstacle for people who want to stay healthy. With a lot of gourmet foods rampant at the night market and elsewhere, it stands to reason that people want to eat them.

2 While consuming those gourmet meals, meals that are high in calories, fats, and sugars, the amount of exercise is not increasing. Before they can come up with an excuse, some people even acknowledge that they do not even exercise at all. Others say that their jobs should take all the blames for their weight because their time is completely occupied by their work. They do not have time to exercise. Therefore, their weight is increasing. Still others go so far as to say it is their kids that make them gain so much weight. Or they do not have P.E. courses.

3 While reading those ridiculous claims of not being responsible for their weight, there are still some people who do care about their own weight. Even though their mind of directing them into exercising does not always triumph psychological urges of eating delicious foods, they take exercise regularly. They do not take elevators either at office buildings or shopping malls. They go to work on foot instead of driving their cars.

4 To sum up, it is irresponsible to shift all the blames to those foods simply because they are absolutely guiltless or simply because you are lazy. It is true that a lack of exercise is the main reason that people have gained so much weight. As long as the level of exercise is in proportion to the amount of food we eat, we do not have to worry about weight gain. So stop blaming them.

  作文中譯加解析

　　我們常說誘惑是最大的敵人，但是將責任都歸到食物上一點幫助都沒有。人們甚至主張了許多荒謬的理由而不用為自己的體重負責。你的看法是？

1 對於想要維持健康的人來說，誘惑是最大的障礙。隨著許多美食在夜市和其他地方應運而生，人們理所當然的想要嚐試。

- 首段定義出誘惑是最大的障礙，人們理所當然的想要嚐試美食，因為美食無所不在。

2 當享用那些富含高卡路里、脂肪和糖的美食餐飲時，但運動的量卻沒有增加。在他們能想出藉口之前，有些人甚至承認他們甚至一點都不運動。有些人說他們的工作該負所有的責任，因為他們的時間都被工作占據了。所以沒有時間運動。因此，他們體重有所增加。還有些人甚至說是他們的小孩讓他們增加了許多體重。亦或是他們又沒有體育課。

- 第二段指出問題所在，當享用那些富含高卡路里、脂肪和糖的美食餐飲時，運動的量卻沒有增加。而且將責任歸咎在其他事情上面更無濟於事。

3 在看到這些為了不用替自己體重負責的荒謬主張的同時，也有些人是在乎自己體重的。即使他們的心理將他們直接引向運動不總是能夠戰勝食用美食的心理衝動，他們規律地運動。他們在辦公大樓或於購物中心時，不會搭電梯。他們步行去上班而非開他們的車。

- 第三段則說明也有些人是在乎自己體重的。也提出具體辦法，例如他們在辦公大樓或於購物中心時，不會搭電梯。他們步行去上班而非開他們的車。

4 總之，將責任都歸咎在食物上是不負責任的，因為食物是無辜的，或只因為你本身是懶惰的。缺乏運動是主因，因為人們增加許多體重。只要運動的等級與我們吃的食物量成正比，我們不必要擔心體重增加。所以停止責備他們。

- 最後總結規避責任是不對的，其實是人本身懶惰。最重要的是運動的等級與我們吃的食物量成正比。

字彙補一補

1. acknowledge **n.** 承認

It's hard for us to acknowledge our fault in front of our kids.

要在我們小孩面前承認自己的錯誤是很難的。

2. exercise **v.** 運動

We need to exercise at least 30 minutes per day.

我們需要每天至少運動三十分鐘。

3. ridiculous **adj.** 荒謬的

It is quite ridiculous to make such a claim.

做那樣的宣稱是相當荒謬的。

4. responsible **adj.** 責任的

We should be responsible for what we eat.

我們該對我們所吃的東西負責。

5. absolutely **adv.** 絕對地

You are absolutely right.

你絕對是對的。

6. gain **v.** 增加

We do not have to step on the scale to learn how much weight we have gained.

我們不需要站在秤上才得知自己體重增加了多少。

Unit 1
Unit 2
Unit 3
Unit 4
Unit 5
Unit 6
Unit 7
Unit 8
Unit 9
Unit 10
Unit 11
Unit 12
Unit 13
Unit 14
Unit 15

重點解析

1. Others say that their jobs should take all the blames for their weight because their time is completely occupied by their work.

   有些人說他們的工作該負所有的責任,因為他們的時間都被工作占據了。

   - others say…表示其他人認為…。
   - take all the blames 表示是承擔所有責任。
   - because 引導副詞子句。
   - is completely occupied by 表示…全然為…佔據了。

2. While reading those ridiculous claims of not being responsible for their weight, there are still some people who do care about their weight.

   在看到這些為了不用替自己體重負責的荒謬主張的同時,也有些人是在乎自己體重的。

   - while 表示當…。
   - be responsible for 表示…負責。
   - there is/there are 為常用的基本句型,其句型後常接代名詞或名詞,再加上時間或地點。
   - who 引導關係代名詞子句,句中為 who do care about their weight 表示在乎他們的體重,其中 do 為加強語氣。

3. Even though their mind of directing them into exercising does not always triumph psychological urges of eating delicious foods, they take exercise regularly.

即使他們的心理將他們直接引向運動不總是能夠戰勝食用美食的心理衝動，他們規律地運動。

- even though 表語氣轉折…，引導副詞子句，其句型為 even though+S+V，S+V（主要子句）。
- directing them into 表示將他們導向為…。
- does not always triumph 表示並不總是勝過。
- psychological urges of eating delicious foods 享用美食的心理衝動。

Unit 14

pull a rabbit out of a hat
拿出一個絕招

 可以這樣寫

1. With the company at stake, we'd better pull a rabbit out of a hat.

   隨著公司在存亡之秋，我們最好拿出絕活來。

2. With the economy in tatters, we must pull a rabbit out of a hat to impress interviewers.

   隨著經濟蕭條，我們必須出其不意才能打動面試官。

句型小貼士

- with 在此表示隨著其用法極為常見，也為常考要點，其為介係詞，常見句型為 With…，S+V…，其後為主要子句。

- pull a rabbit out of a hat …指作出讓周遭驚豔之舉，引申為拿出一個絕招（不同凡響的解決辦法）/出其不意的意思。

- at stake 指在危及/危險中，其引申為在存亡之秋。

- with the economy in tatters 指隨著經濟蕭條。

⚡ 句型腦激盪

★With the company at stake, our CEO said that we'd better pull a rabbit out of a hat.

⇨With the company at stake, our outstanding CEO said that we'd better pull a rabbit out of a hat.

隨著公司在存亡之秋，我們傑出的首席執行長說我們最好拿出絕活來。

★With the economy in tatters, a CFO wishes we could pull a rabbit out of a hat so that situations will not be worsened.

⇨With the economy in tatters, an accomplished CFO wishes we could pull a rabbit out of a hat so that situations will not be worsened.

隨著經濟蕭條，有才華的首席財務長希望我們最好拿出本領來，情況才得以免於惡化。

★An accountant pulls a rabbit out of a hat, so the company can effortlessly deal with those officials.

⇨An accountant with great enthusiasm pulls a rabbit out of a hat, so the company can effortlessly deal with those officials.

具熱忱的會計師拿出了絕活，所以公司能不費吹灰之力地應付那些官員。

★We should pull a rabbit out of a hat so that a general manager cannot find fault with us.

⇨We should pull a rabbit out of a hat so that a general manager with a bad intention cannot find fault with us.

我們最好拿出絕活來，這樣有不良意圖的總經理才不能找我們麻煩。

★A salesperson pulls a rabbit out of a hat and really saves the day.

⇨A salesperson who knows how to sell pulls a rabbit out of a hat and really saves the day.

懂得如何銷售的銷售人員拿出絕活來救了大家。

★An assistant manager pulls a rabbit out of a hat, so the profit of the company improves significantly.

⇨An assistant manager with a persistent goal pulls a rabbit out of a hat, so the profit of the company improves significantly.

有著堅定目標的副經理拿出了絕活來，所以公司的利潤有了大幅地改進。

★The auditor pulls a rabbit out of a hat, so the police cannot find anything.

⇨The auditor who knows how to cover pulls a rabbit out of a hat, so the police cannot find anything.

知道如何能掩飾的審計師拿出了絕活，所以警方找不到任何東西。

★The designer pulled a rabbit out of a hat, so the runway finale can be so terrific.

⇨The designer who has great talent pulled a rabbit out of a hat, so the runway finale can be so terrific.

這個十分有才華的設計師拿出了絕活，所以伸展台終場可以這麼棒。

★The Chief Accountant pulls a rabbit out of a hat, so we can leave office early.

⇨The super nice Chief Accountant pulls a rabbit out of a hat, so we can leave office early.

人超好的總會計主任拿出了絕活所以我們能提早離開辦公室。

★A senior clerk pulls a rabbit out of a hat, so managers give him a year-end bonus.

⇨A senior clerk who always can impresses all colleagues, pulls a rabbit out of a hat, so managers give him a year-end bonus.

一位總是令所有同事印象深刻的高級職員拿出了絕活，所以經理們給了他年終獎金。

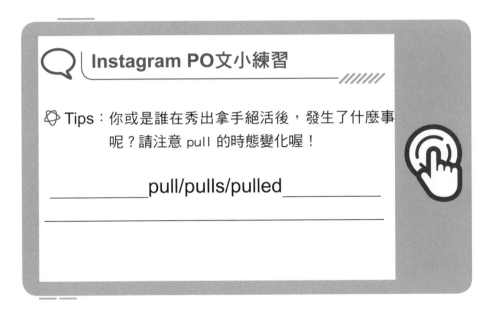

Q Instagram PO文小練習

⊛ Tips：你或是誰在秀出拿手絕活後，發生了什麼事呢？請注意 pull 的時態變化喔！

_____pull/pulls/pulled_____

_____

作文範例

Increasing dependence on smartphone, social networking sites, and many other things have led us to rethink the development of the new technology. Some are shifting all the blames to this development, especially the Internet bullying, claiming that it has a negative influence on our lives. What is your opinion?

1 Nowadays, advanced technology has certainly made our lives more comfortable and convenient, but with many devices being developed, it has affected how people behave and how people interact with each other.

2 The prevalence of using smartphones and related devices has led to the emergence of social networking sites. The increasing dependence for the smartphone and these sites has given rise to the alienation among people. During family or friend gatherings, people used to have an adequate amount of greetings and chats, but people now scroll the smartphones all the time, taking their own photos as if others were invisible. In the workplace, the phenomenon is prevalent, too. Instead of actually having a real meeting, people like to use Skype or Facebook to convey messages.

It is faster sometimes, but often messages have been mis-read. It takes a lot more time for each division to reach a consensus. A lot of issues can be readily solved right on the spot if anyone seems to have a problem with those.

3 People now have a feeling that they are not as close as they used to. Of course, there is nothing wrong with using these devices, but these devices have turned people into a cold machine. After all, we are humans. There is still a need for one to form a real friendship and has a real communication face-to-face.

4 To sum up, even if advanced technology has provided us with more ways to interact with others, most people cannot properly use this device. Most important of all, how can you expect heavy users of smartphones to admit the fact that smartphones indeed have a negative influence on their lives. I think the answer you will probably get is "see I'm still talking to you" for one second, but their eyes move directly to the smartphone for the next few seconds. Unless you <u>pull a rabbit out of a hat</u> to remove their eyes from the smart-phone, their eyes will still linger on the smartphone.

作文中譯加解析

> 對於逐漸仰賴智慧型手機、社交網站、和許多其他事，已使得我們重新思考新科技的發展。有些人把責任都歸到這個發展上，尤其是網路霸凌，聲稱這對我們的生活是有負面影響的。你的看法是？

1. 現今，先進科技確實已讓我們的生活更舒適且更為方便，但是隨著許多裝置的進展已影響到人們如何表現和人們彼此的互動。

   - 首段先定義出先進科技確實已讓我們的生活更舒適且更為方便，並指出隨著許多裝置的進展已影響到人們如何表現和人們彼此的互動。

2. 使用智慧型手機和相關裝置的普及已使得社群網站的浮現。逐漸仰賴智慧型手機和這些網站已導致人們之間的疏離。在家庭或朋友聚會中，人們過去有適切的問候和交談，但人們現在總是在滑手機，拍他們自己的照片，彷彿其他人是不存在的。在職場上，這個現象是普遍的。人們喜歡用 skype 或臉書傳達訊息，而非實際開會。於某些時候是快速的，但是通常訊息是被誤讀的。對每個部門來說是需花費更多時間達成共識。很多議題需要當場立即解決，如果每個人對那些都有問題的話。

   - 第二段說明並指出問題逐漸仰賴智慧型手機和這些網站已導致人們之間的疏離。除了家庭聚會外，也以在職場為例，有時候導致更嚴重的問題，通常訊息是被誤讀的。有時候需花費更多時間達成共識。而且很多議題需要當場立即解決。

3 人們現在有種感覺，即是他們不再像過去那樣親密。當然使用這些裝置沒有錯，但是這些裝置已使得人們成為冷酷的機器。畢竟我們是人類。真實的友誼是有需要的且需要實際的面對面溝通。

- 第二段說明人們現在有種感覺，即是他們不在像過去那樣親密。並指出實際面對面溝通是必須的。

4 總之，即使先進科技已提供我們與他人互動得更多方法，大多數人無法適當的使用這裝置。更重要的是，你如何能夠期待智慧型手機的重度使用者，承認智慧型手機對於他們的生活有負面的影響。我認為你會得到的答案是這秒回答你看吧我仍在跟你講話，而下一秒眼睛就直接轉移到智慧型手機上。除非你能拿出本領來讓他們目光移開智慧型手機，他們的目光仍流連在智慧型手機上。

- 最後總結出大多數人無法適當的使用這裝置。並反諷你如何能夠期待智慧型手機的重度使用者，承認智慧型手機對於他們的生活有負面的影響。最後以幽默的方式結束本文。

字彙補一補

1. comfortable **adj.** 舒適的
   The backstage is just as comfortable as the front stage.
   後台就如同前端舞台一樣舒適。

2. convenient **adj.** 方便的
   It is convenient for us to use the chopsticks eat Chinese dishes.
   對我們來說以筷子食用中國餐點是方便的。

3. prevalence **n.** 普及
   The prevalence of the smartphone is an interesting phenomenon.
   智慧型手機的普及是有趣的現象。

4. emergence **n.** 出現
   Emergence of super stars has aroused a lot of screaming.
   巨星的出現已引起許多尖叫。

5. alienation **n.** 疏離感
   She feels a sense of alienation after having a fight with her husband.
   在與她丈夫吵架後，她感到疏離感。

6. invisible **adj.** 看不見的
   Bacteria are invisible with a naked eye.
   細菌用肉眼是看不見的。

重點解析

1. The increasing dependence for the smartphone and these sites has given rise to the alienation among people.

逐漸仰賴智慧型手機和這些網站已導致人們之間的疏離。

- increasing dependence 表示逐漸仰賴。
- give rise to 表示導致…。
- alienation among people 表示人們之間的疏離感。

2. During family or friend gatherings, people used to have an adequate amount of greetings and chats, but people now scroll the smartphones all the time, taking their own photos as if others were invisible.

在家庭或朋友聚會中,人們過去有適切的問候和交談,但人們現在總是在滑手機,拍他們自己的照片,彷彿其他人是不存在的。

- during family or friend gatherings 表示在家庭或朋友聚會期間。
- used to 表示過去是…。
- as if 表示彷彿…,引導副詞子句,其句型為 As if +S+V, S+V(主要子句)。
- an adequate amount of greetings and chats 表示適量的問候跟聊天。

3. Of course, there is nothing wrong with using these devices, but these devices have turned people into a cold machine.

當然使用這些裝置沒有錯，但是這些裝置已使得人們成為冷酷的機器。

- of course…表示當然。
- there is/there are 為常用的基本句型，其句型後常接代名詞或名詞，在加上時間或地點，there is nothing wrong with 表示這樣沒有什麼不對。
- turn into 表示…轉變成…。
- have turned people into a cold machine.已將人們轉成冷酷的機器。

Instagram
PO 文+寫作高級篇

when
當…的時候

 可以這樣寫

1. When you are stuck in the middle, you should stay positive and calm.

   當你進退兩難時,你應該保持積極正面且鎮定。

2. When members of the entire marketing department have a feeling that they are stuck in the middle, they try not to be pessimistic.

   當整個行銷部門的成員有種他們處於進退兩難的感覺時,他們嘗試不悲觀思考。

句型小貼士

- when 表示當…其用法極為常見,也為常考要點,其為表時間的從屬連接詞引導副詞子句,常見句型為 When S+V…,S+V…,其後為主要子句。

- stuck in the middle 引申為卡在中間/進退兩難。

- have a feeling 表示有種…感覺。

- try not to 表示嘗試不…,not 為否定詞置於 to 前。

152

[⚡] 句型腦激盪

★When the CEO is deliberating the final candidate with other managers, all candidates are very nervous.

⇨When the outstanding CEO is deliberating the final candidate with other managers, all candidates are very nervous.

當傑出首席執行長與其他經理們正在商議最終候選人，所有的候選人都感到緊張。

★When a CFO is promoted to the higher position, the vacancy is still pending.

⇨When an accomplished CFO is promoted to the higher position, the vacancy is still pending.

當首席財務長升遷到更高的職位，職位空缺卻仍懸而未決。

★When an accountant encounters an obstacle, he will not feel defeated.

⇨When an accountant with great enthusiasm encounters an obstacle, he will not feel defeated.

當具熱忱的會計師犯了錯，他不會有受挫感。

★When a general manager tries to manipulate someone, he will try to be nice to you on the surface.

⇨When a general manager with a bad intention tries to manipulate someone, he will try to be nice to you on the surface.

當意圖不良的總經理試圖操控某人，他會試著在表面上對你很好。

★When a salesperson closes a deal, he bursts out laughing.

⇨When a salesperson who knows how to sell closes a deal, he bursts out laughing.

當懂得如何銷售的銷售人員又成交了一筆交易，他仰天長笑。

★When an assistant manager meets the need of the client, he knows that he will soon be promoted.

⇨When an assistant manager with a persistent goal meets the need of the client, he knows that he will soon be promoted.

當具堅定目標的副經理達到客戶的需求時，他知道自己即將升遷。

★When the auditor gets caught, he is going to pay for what he did.

⇨When the auditor who covered up mistakes gets caught, he is going to pay for what he did.

當掩飾錯誤的審計師被抓到時，他將為自己所作所為負責。

★When designers are discussing their views, the reporter rudely interrupts them.

⇨When designers with a great vision are discussing their views, the reporter rudely interrupts them.

當具遠見的設計師們正討論他們的觀點時，記者莽撞地打斷他們。

★When the Chief Accountant knows that there is an overseas position in the rival company, he tries to contact the poaching company.

⇨When the Chief Accountant who didn't get the desired position last month, knows that there is an overseas position in the rival company, he tries to contact the poaching company.

總會計主任上個月沒有得到想要的職位，當他得知競爭公司有個海外職缺，他試圖與獵人頭公司接洽。

★When a senior clerk fails to convince the client, his confidence immediately drops.

⇨When a senior clerk who always impresses our clients, fails to convince the client, his confidence immediately drops.

當總令人印象深刻的高級職員無法說服客戶，他的信心立即下滑。

Unit 15
Unit 16
Unit 17
Unit 18
Unit 19
Unit 20
Unit 21
Unit 22
Unit 23
Unit 24
Unit 25
Unit 26
Unit 27
Unit 28

💬 **Instagram PO文小練習**

⚛ Tips：請試著寫下當你做了某事之後的感受是怎樣的呢？

When _____

_____

作文範例

> *With new technology being developed, our lives have been influenced significantly. Whether it is good or bad, the way people greet with one another has changed. This has affected our relationships with others. What is your opinion?*

1 Nowadays, advanced technology has certainly made our lives more comfortable and convenient, but with many devices being developed, it has affected how people behave and how people interact with each other.

2 Not all people are borne with an extrovert personality. For most introverts, the development and invention of many social networking sites are a godsend. They do not have to worry how should I respond to this question, what should I do, or did I say it correctly. With these devices being developed, they have an excuse of saying, oh sorry I don't see it. Most of the time, they do need more time to think. Using these devices does provide them with plenty of time to prepare the answers. It is totally a lifesaver for an introvert when responding to others.

3 Furthermore, words and messages have been replaced by photos or pictures. It is a new way for people to have a greeting or start a conversation with others. It is kind of fun sending people Line pictures indicating a New Year greeting rather than simply saying "hey Happy New Year" in a phone. This is a new trend of forming a relationship with family members, friends, and Internet friends. Also, there are clubs on those sites. People with the similar interests can share things with one another. Messages can be instantly exchanged. Problems could probably be easily solved if you post it on your Facebook wall. These are all the advantages of using social networking sites.

4 To sum up, from all the above-mentioned advantages, it can clearly be seen that technology has a positive influence on our lives. It is an elevated version of relationship-forming.

作文中譯加解析

隨著新科技的開發，我們的生活已大幅地受到影響。不論是好或壞，人們與其他人的問候方式也改變了。這也影響到我們與其他人的關係。你的看法是？

1 現今，先進的科技確實已使得我們的生活更舒適且方便，但隨著許多裝置的開發，這已經影響到人們如何表現和人們如何與彼此互動。

• 首段先定義科技對生活的影響，也指出隨著許多裝置的開發，這已經影響到人們如何表現和人們如何與彼此互動。

2 並非所有人都與生俱有外向的性格。對大多數內向的人來說，許多社群網站的開發和發明是天賜。他們不用擔心該如何回應問題，思考著我們該如何做或我這麼說是正確的嗎？隨著這些裝置的開發，他們有正當藉口說，喔！抱歉我沒看到。大多數時候他們是需要更多時間去思考的。使用這些裝置也給了他們許多時間去準備答案。當內向的人在回應別人時，這全然是個救星。

• 第二段說明並非所有人都與生俱有外向的性格。並以內向的人為例，說明這些裝置對內向者帶來的好處。對內向者來說這真的是個救星。

3 此外，文字和訊息也已經被照片或圖像取代。對人們來說，這是與人問候或開啟交談的新方式。傳送象徵著新年快樂問候的 line 圖片，而非僅於電話中說嗨新年快樂，是挺有趣的。這對於與家庭成員朋友和網友構成一段關係是個新的趨勢。而且，那些網站上有不同的社團。有相同興趣的人，能彼此共享事物。訊息能即刻交換。問題可能會輕而易舉地被解決，如果你將它發佈到你的臉書牆上。這些都是使用社群網站的優點。

- 第三段說明了使用社群網站的優點。某種程度上，文字和訊息也已經被照片或圖像取代。人們可以用更有趣的方式來問候友人，訊息能即刻交換。有相同興趣的人，能彼此共享事物。

4 總之，從上述優點來看，能清楚看出科技對我們生活是有助益的。這是形成新關係的升級版。

- 最後總結出科技對我們生活是有助益的。

字彙補一補

1. advanced **adj.** 先進的
   Computer software in this school is advanced.
   這間學校的電腦軟體是先進的。

2. extrovert **adj.** 外向的
   An extrovert personality is so endearing.
   外向的個性是如此討人喜歡的。

3. invention **n.** 發明
   The invention of the social networking sites is good for our society.
   社群網站的發明對我們社會是好的。

4. respond **v.** 回應
   Knowing how to respond to the customer is very vital.
   懂得如何回應客戶是很重要的。

5. conversation **n.** 會話
   If you don't know how to start a conversation with your date, you can consult some books.
   如果你不懂得如何與你的約會對象展開交談，你可以參考一些書。

6. messages **n.** 訊息
   Messages sometimes have been misread by most of us.
   有些時候我們大多數的人都將訊息誤讀了。

重點解析

Unit 15
Unit 16
Unit 17
Unit 18
Unit 19
Unit 20
Unit 21
Unit 22
Unit 23
Unit 24
Unit 25
Unit 26
Unit 27
Unit 28

1. They do not have to worry how should I respond to this question, what should I do, or did I say it correctly.

他們不用擔心該如何回應問題，思考著我們該如何做或我這麼說是正確的嗎？

- do not have to worry 表示不用擔心。
- how should I respond to this question 表示他們不用擔心該如何回應問題。
- what should I do 表示我該如何做。
- or did I say it correctly 表示或我這麼說是正確的嗎。

2. It is kind of fun sending people Line pictures indicating a New Year greeting rather than simply saying "hey Happy New Year" in a phone.

傳送象徵著新年快樂問候的 line 圖片，而非僅於電話中說嗨新年快樂，是挺有趣的。

- sending people Line pictures 表示傳 Line 照片給人。
- rather than 表示而不是，與 instead of 常用。
- There is/there are 為常用的基本句型，其句型後常接代名詞或名詞，再加上時間或地點。
- that 引導關係代名詞子句，句中為 indicating a New Year greeting，indicating 由 that indicate 簡化而來，表示象徵新年問候。

3. Problems could probably be easily solved if you post it on your Facebook wall.

問題可能會輕而易舉地被解決，如果你將它發佈到你的臉書牆上。

- problems can be easily solved 表示問題可以輕易解決。
- if 表示如果…，引導副詞子句，其句型為 If+S+V，S+V（主要子句）。
- post it on 表示發佈在…。
- on your Facebook wall 表示在臉書牆上。

A list
A 咖、一流的

可以這樣寫

1. The company is not large enough to hire an A list designer.

   公司沒有大到能雇用一流的設計師。

2. Our firm truly needs an A list salesperson to boost our sale.

   我們公司真的需要一流的銷售人員,以增加我們的銷售。

句型小貼士

- enough to 表示足夠…/能…其用法極為常見,需注意 enough 置於副詞和形容詞後。

- an A list 表示「一流的」,可做為形容詞及名詞。

- not large enough 表示沒有大到…,not 置於 large enough 前。

句型腦激盪

★We certainly cannot handle those financial problems without an A list CFO.

⇨We certainly cannot handle those financial problems without an A list CFO who has confidence in himself.

沒有對自己充滿自信的一流首席財務長，我們確實無法處理那些財務問題。

★An A list Accountant certainly has plenty of options in job-finding.

⇨An A list Accountant who has excellent work experience certainly has plenty of options in job-finding.

有極佳工作經驗的一流會計師在找工作時有許多選擇。

★An A list General Manager equals tremendous profits.

⇨An A list capable General Manager equals tremendous profits.

一流、有能力的總經理等同於巨大的利益。

★It is hard to find an A list salesperson.

⇨It is hard to find an A list salesperson who's reliable.

很難找到可信賴的一流銷售人員。

★An A list assistant manager will soon replace the manager.

⇨An A list assistant manager with great honesty will soon replace the manager.

一流又誠實的副經理很快會取代經理。

★An A list auditor certainly knows how to do multiple things simultaneously.

⇨An A list experienced auditor certainly knows how to do multiple things simultaneously.

一流又有經驗的審計師的確懂得如何同時做許多事。

★An A list designer will earn a lot of money.

⇨An A list designer with tremendous social skills will earn a lot of money.

一個一流且又會打好人際關係的設計師會賺很多錢。

★An overseas position is offered to an A list Chief Accountant.

⇨An A list overseas position is offered to the A list Chief Accountant.

一流的總會計主任得到一份 A 級的海外工作職缺。

★An A list senior clerk is not satisfied with his income.

⇨An A list senior clerk is not satisfied with his B list income.

一流的高級職員不滿意他的 B 級收入。

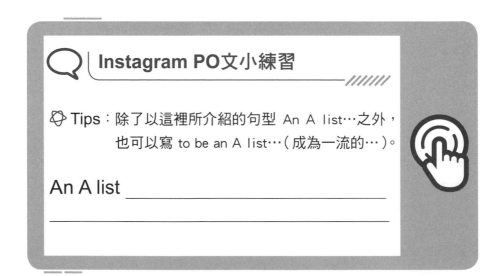

Instagram PO文小練習

⚛ Tips：除了以這裡所介紹的句型 An A list…之外，
也可以寫 to be an A list…（成為一流的…）。

An A list _____

_____

作文範例

/////////

Most people might have a feeling that there has been increasing traffic and pollution problems than it used to be. Some claim that the use of gasoline and petroleum is the main cause, and problems can be solved if we increase the price of gasoline and petroleum used for all purposes. What is your idea? What is the possible solution?

1 Increasing the price of petrol is not the best way to solve growing traffic and pollution problems. It will make our lives miserable.

2 Even if price of petrol is increased, there is still a need for all of us. It is relevant to all our daily necessities. Devising other efficient transportation facilities and developing other sustainable, non-polluted, renewable energy resources are the long-term solutions. Unless these facilities and other energy resources are developed, traffic and pollution problems still remain.

3 These days, with soaring petrol prices and many other things, some people do take other means of transportation to work or travel. But still lots of people drive their car to work. There is nothing they can do because they do not have an electric car or cars that use other non-polluted energy resources.

4 However, despite with all these, governments have been working on several ways, hoping that these problems will be solved. One of the most effective ways is having the U-bike around the MRT stations or campuses. Some people who used to drive to work now take the U-bike plus MRT to work. It somehow reduces the use of traffic. Another way is to speed up the MRT construction. With more routes being built, people can even take MRT to the International airport without taking a taxi or having their relatives gave them a ride. The commute time, traffic and pollution problems can be significantly reduced given the numbers of people who take an airplane in a single day.

5 To sum up, I believe with all these above-mentioned measures, we do not have to be an A list expert to know the problem, and all problems will be solved in the future, but increasing petrol and gasoline price is definitely not one of them.

作文中譯加解析

Unit 15
Unit 16
Unit 17
Unit 18
Unit 19
Unit 20
Unit 21
Unit 22
Unit 23
Unit 24
Unit 25
Unit 26
Unit 27
Unit 28

　　許多人可能有種感覺，比起過往交通和汙染的問題持續增加。有人宣稱使用汽油和石油是主因。問題能被解決如果我們增加石油和汽油用於各種用途的價格。你的想法是？可能的解決之道是？

1 增加石油和汽油價格不是解決交通和汙染問題增長的最佳解決之道。這只會使得我們的生活更悲慘。

- 首段先定義增加石油和汽油價格不是解決交通和汙染問題增長的最佳解決之道。

2 即使石油和汽油的價格增加，對我們大多數的人來說仍是有需求的。這與我們所有每日各項需求有關。設計其他有效率的交通設施和發展其他永續，無汙染，且再生能源的資源是長期解決之道。除非這些設施和其他能源資源已開發，交通和汙染問題仍存在。

- 第二段說明需求性，更表明設計其他有效率的交通設施和發展其他永續和無汙染且再生能源的資源是長期解決之道，不然交通和汙染問題會持續存在。

3 這些日子，隨著高漲的石油和汽油價格和許多其他東西，有些人確實搭乘其他交通工具上班或旅行。但仍有許多人仍開他們的車上班。他們並不能做什麼，因為他們沒有電子車或使用其他沒有汙染的能源資源的車子。

- 第三段說明人們因為石油價格等改以其他方式去上班或旅行。

4 然而，儘管隨著這些，政府已經在幾個方面上努力，期許這些問題
能有所解決。其中一個最有效的方式是在校園或捷運附近設置 U-
bike。有些人過去是開車上班的，現在改以搭乘 U-bike 和捷運上
班。這某些程度上降低了交通的使用。另一個方式是，加速捷運的
建造。隨著更多路線的建立，人們甚至可以搭乘捷運到國際機場沒
有搭乘計程車或需要他們的親戚載他們一乘。通勤時間和交通問題
能大幅地降低，考量到人們單日搭乘到機場的數量。

- 第四段說明政府的努力，也提出了解決方法，其中一個是在校園
  或捷運附近設置 U-bike。幾種交通工具的結合，使得通勤時間
  和交通問題能大幅地降低。

5 總之我相信隨著這些上述措施，我們不需要成為一流的專家才知道
問題，所有問題在未來都能有所解決但增加石油和汽油價格卻絕不
是他們其中一個。

- 最後總結出問題始終能得到解決。

字彙補一補

Unit 15
Unit 16
Unit 17
Unit 18
Unit 19
Unit 20
Unit 21
Unit 22
Unit 23
Unit 24
Unit 25
Unit 26
Unit 27
Unit 28

1. relevant **adj.** 相關的

This is relevant to the growth of the company.

這與公司的成長有關。

2. efficient **adj.** 有效的

Developing an efficient means of the transportation system is not easy.

開發出有效率的交通系統不容易。

3. sustainable **adj.** 永續利用的

Sustainable development is important for us.

永續發展對我們來說是重要的。

4. non-polluted **adj.** 無汙染的

The non-polluted fruits, although not as pretty as the other fruit, are the healthiest ones.

無汙染的水果，儘管沒有其他水果看起來漂亮，是最健康的水果。

5. campuses **n.** 校園

The campuses are full of lots of activities during the Christmas.

在聖誕節期間校園充滿了許多活動。

6. commute **n.** 通勤

The commute time is one of the considerations for many jobseekers.

通勤時間是許多找工作的人的考量之一。

重點解析

1. Devising other efficient transportation facilities and developing other sustainable, non-polluted, renewable energy resources are the long-term solutions.

設計其他有效率的交通設施和發展其他永續, 無汙染, 且再生能源的資源是長期解決之道。

- "Devising other efficient transportation facilities and developing other sustainable, non-polluted, renewable energy resources" 為動名詞當主詞，其中 devising 為 v1 而 developing 為 v2，中間以 and 連接。
- other efficient transportation facilities 表示其它有效率的交通設施。
- other sustainable, non-polluted, renewable energy resources 表示其它永續利用、無汙染、再生能源資源。
- long-term solutions 表示長期的解決之道。

2. However, despite with all these, governments have been working on several ways, hoping that these problems will be solved.

然而，儘管隨著這些，政府已經在幾個方面上努力，期許這些問題能有所解決。

- however 表語氣轉折⋯表示然而。
- despite 為介詞，despite with all these 表示儘管所有這些⋯。
- have been working on 為現在進行式表示一直在努力中。
- these problems will be solved 表示這些問題會解決。

3. The commute time, traffic and pollution problems can be significantly reduced given the numbers of people who take an airplane in a single day.

通勤時間和交通問題能大幅地降低，考量到人們單日搭乘到機場的數量。

- can be significantly reduced 表示能大幅地降低。
- given 表示考量到…。
- the numbers of people 表示數量。
- who 引導關係代名詞子句，句中為 take an airplane in a single day 表示一天內搭乘飛機的人。

 可以這樣寫

1. The soil is brimming with 14 essential nutrients.
   土壤富含著 14 種必須營養素。

2. Our country is not brimming with voices that are outdated.
   我們國家不全是過時的聲音。

句型小貼士

- be brimming with 表示…充滿，為極常見的用法。

- 表示…充滿有其他同義用法如 be filled with 和 be full of 於高中課本中常見，而 be brimming with 和 be laden with 則於雜誌或短文小品中常出現。

- 例句 2 的 voices 後又以關係代名詞 that 作為延伸句。

句型腦激盪

★On-line games are not brimming with violence and sex.

⇨On-line games are not entirely brimming with violence and sex.

線上遊戲不全是充滿著暴力和性。

★Night market foods are not brimming with plenty of choices.

⇨Night market foods are not necessarily brimming with plenty of choices.

夜市食物並不總是充滿著許多選擇。

★Company restaurants are not brimming with people.

⇨Company restaurants are not always brimming with people.

公司餐廳並不總是充滿著人。

★Theaters are brimming with moviegoers.

⇨Theaters are usually brimming with moviegoers.

戲院總是充滿著電影愛好者。

★Churches are not necessarily brimming with people.

⇨Churches are not necessarily brimming with people who genuinely want to be there.

教堂並不總是充滿著真心地想要在那的人。

★Campus new coffee shops are brimming with students.

⇨Campus new coffee shops are brimming with students who want to free from the torture of the heat wave.

校園新咖啡店充滿著想要免於熱浪折磨的學生。

★Amusement parks are brimming with crowds.

⇨Amusement parks are brimming with crowds who want to have an unforgettable vacation.

遊樂園充滿著想要有難忘回憶的人群。

★Museums are brimming with students.

⇨Museums are brimming with students who have to write statue evaluation homework.

博物館充滿必須寫雕像評估作業的學生。

★Hotels are brimming with tourists.

⇨Hotels are brimming with tourists who have their flight delayed.

旅館充滿著受班機延誤的旅客。

★Department stores are brimming with people.

⇨Department stores are brimming with people who want to buy clothes at the discounted price.

百貨公司充滿著想要以折扣價格購買衣服的人。

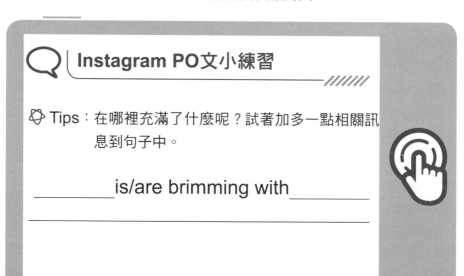

💬 | **Instagram PO文小練習**

🔀 Tips：在哪裡充滿了什麼呢？試著加多一點相關訊
　　　息到句子中。

_____is/are brimming with_____

_____

作文範例

It's often said that temptations are the greatest enemy. It seems that people in all ages are gaining weight, and this has influenced overall public health. What is your opinion? And what is the solution?

1 Temptations are the great obstacle for people who want to stay healthy. Places that are brimming with gourmet foods are the greatest hindrance for us to stay healthy. With a lot of gourmet foods rampant on the night market and elsewhere, it stands to reason that people want to eat them. No wonder people have gained so much weight.

2 However, the level of exercise is not in proportion to the amount of food we eat. Moreover, people consume more calories than we need. It is irresponsible to say that our stomach still has a room for snacks and other gourmet meals even if we are full. Although the statement is true, it has exceeded our daily calories consumption.

3 Staying away from junk foods seems to be the solution of not consuming foods that contain so many calories and sugars. Setting a scheme of eating at home and the frequency of eating those foods might help a little bit. Furthermore, we have to build a healthy lifestyle and have a regular eating habit. Our lifestyle and habits will play a significant role on the frequency at which we consume certain food, so this is essential for us to develop this kind of behavior, especially at the early age of childhood.

4 Studies also have found that people with a healthy lifestyle tend to have a slim figure whether they exercise or not. It seems that exercising play a minimum role in weight-gaining. The point is if you do not have the healthy lifestyle, no matter how hard you exercise, you are still in an overweight circle.

5 To sum up, from the above mentioned points, developing a healthy lifestyle and forming a good eating habit are the solution to the overweight problem. You will be surprised when your friends look at you and comment on how you manage to keep a slim figure.

作文中譯加解析

我們常說誘惑是最大的敵人。似乎所有年齡層的人都增胖了，這影響了大眾健康。你的看法是？而解決之道是？

1 對於想要維持健康的人來說，誘惑是最大的障礙。充滿美食的地方對我們來說是個很大的障礙。隨著許多美食在夜市和其他地方應運而生，人們理所當然的想要嘗試。難怪人們增加了許多重量。

- 首段先定義對於想要維持健康的人來說，誘惑是最大的障礙。這也使得人們想要嘗試那些食物進而使體重增加。

2 然而，我們所吃的食物量與所運動的程度是不成比例的。此外，人們攝取了比我們所需要的量更多的卡路里。而述說我們的胃總有放甜食和其他美食餐飲的空間，即使我們已經飽了，是不負責任的。雖然這些陳述是真的，但是它已超過得我們每日消耗的卡路里。

- 第二段說明我們所吃的食物量與所運動的程度是不成比例的。而其他陳述是很荒謬的，而且這些美食已超過得我們每日消耗的卡路里。

3 遠離垃圾食物似乎是不攝取含有許多卡路里跟糖的食物的解決之道。制定在家飲食的計劃和食用那些食物的頻率可能有些許幫助。此外，我們必須建立一個健康的生活模式且養成規律的飲食習慣。我們的生活方式跟習慣將對我們消費特定食物的頻率扮演重要的角色，所以這對我們發展這種行為，由其是於孩童時期初期，是很重要的。

- 第三段説明解決之道,並表明制定在家飲食的計劃和食用那些食物的頻率可能有些許幫助。養成一個健康的生活模式且養成規律的飲食習慣也是很重要的。

4 研究也已經發現具有健康生活方式的人傾向有更苗條的體態,不論他們運動與否。似乎運動在體重增加方面扮演著較不重要的角色。重點是如果你不具有健康的生活方式,不論你如何運動,仍會處於肥胖的循環。

- 第四段説明研究也已經發現具有健康生活方式的人傾向有更苗條的體態,但若不具有健康的生活方式,不論你如何運動,仍會處於肥胖的循環。

5 總之,從上述觀點,發展健康的生活方式和養成良好的飲食習慣是體重增加問題的解決之道。你將感到驚訝當你的朋友注視著你,評論著你如何設法保持著苗條的身材。

- 作出總結,發展健康的生活方式和養成良好的飲食習慣是體重增加問題的解決之道。

字彙補一補

1. temptation **n.** 誘惑
We are faced with lots of temptations while walking down the street.
當走在街頭上，我們面臨許多誘惑。

2. rampant **adj.** 蔓延的
Numerous diseases are rampant in the war zone.
在戰區許多疾病正蔓延著。

3. healthy **adj.** 健康的
We need to stay healthy to enjoy our life.
我們需要維持健康以享受我們的生活。

4. proportion **n.** 比例
The number of beverages we drink is not in proportion to the amount of water we metabolize.
我們飲入的飲料數量與我們代謝掉的水的量不成正比。

5. lifestyle **n.** 生活方式
A sedentary lifestyle will not do us any good.
久坐的生活方式對我們來說沒任何助益。

6. overweight **adj.** 過重的
Some people are so lucky that they do not have to worry an overweight problem.
有些人很幸運他們不用擔憂體重過重的問題。

重點解析

1. With a lot of gourmet foods rampant on the night market and elsewhere, it stands to reason that people want to eat them.

隨著許多美食在夜市和其他地方應運而生，人們理所當然的想要嘗試。

- with 為介系詞，此處句型為 With…，S+V 的句型。
- that 引導關係代名詞子句，在句中省略了 that are，成為 With a lot of gourmet foods rampant on the night market and elsewhere 表示隨著許多美食蔓延在夜市和其他地方。
- it stands to reason that…表示理所當然的是…。

2. Staying away from junk foods seems to be the solution of not consuming foods that contain so many calories and sugars.

遠離垃圾食物似乎是不攝取含有許多卡路里跟糖的食物的解決之道。

- staying away from junk foods…表示遠離垃圾食物為動名詞當主詞，其後加單數動詞 seems。
- the solution of not consuming foods 表示不攝取食物的解決之道。
- that 引導關係代名詞子句，句中為 that contain so many calories and sugars 表示含許多卡路里跟糖。

3. Studies also have found that people with a healthy lifestyle tend to have a slim figure whether they exercise or not.

研究也已經發現具有健康生活方式的人傾向有更苗條的體態，不論他們運動與否。

- studies also have found 表示研究發現…。
- people with a healthy lifestyle 表示具健康生活方式的人。
- tend to 表示傾向於…。
- a slim figure 表示苗條身材。
- whether they exercise or not 表示不論他們運動與否。

 可以這樣寫

/////////

1. Mark is surprised to learn that Jennifer is a 3S lady.

   得知珍妮佛是剩女讓馬克很驚訝。

2. Clients are surprised to learn that Ann is a mom of 5 children.

   客戶對於安是五個孩子的媽媽感到驚訝。

句型小貼士

- 分詞是由動詞變化而來的,可分為現在分詞和過去分詞。

- surprised 於句中當主詞補語,修飾主詞 Mark 和 clients,且為分詞當形容詞的用法。

- A 3S lady 表示到了適婚年齡卻沒結婚的女性也就是指剩女,為極常見的用法。

⚡ 句型腦激盪

★Mark is surprised to learn that his wife's brother won a world championship.

⇨Mark is surprised to learn that his wife's brother won a world championship in his early twenties.

得知他老婆的弟弟在 20 幾歲出頭時就贏得一項世界冠軍讓馬克感到很驚訝。

★Mark is surprised to learn that his boss is a woman.

⇨Mark is surprised to learn that his boss is a woman in her thirties.

得知他的老闆是 30 幾歲的女士讓馬克很驚訝。

★Mark is surprised to learn that he is a boy.

⇨Mark is surprised to learn that he is just a teenage boy.

得知他是一個 10 幾歲的男孩讓馬克很驚訝。

★Mark is surprised to learn that Jon is a girl.

⇨Mark is surprised to learn that Jon is a girl with a great countenance.

得知瓊是一個具有良好面容的女孩讓馬克很驚訝。

★Mark is surprised to learn that he is a businessman.

⇨Mark is surprised to learn that he is a businessman with a promising future.

得知他是具前途光明的商人讓馬克很驚訝。

★Mark is surprised to learn that Jennifer is a detective.

⇨Mark is surprised to learn that Jennifer is a detective with a dark smile.

得知珍妮佛是帶有陰暗笑容的警探讓馬克很驚訝。

★Mark is surprised to find out that his best friends' father is a cop.
⇨Mark is surprised to find out that his best friends' father is a handsome cop.

得知他最好的朋友的父親是英俊的警察讓馬克很驚訝。

★Mark is surprised to know that his neighbor is a blind man.
⇨Mark is surprised to know that his neighbor is a blind man with a kind heart.

得知他的鄰居是具有好心腸的盲人讓馬克很驚訝。

★Mark is surprised to learn that Jennifer is a beautiful woman.
⇨Mark is surprised to learn that Jennifer is a beautiful woman with a malicious heart.

得知珍妮佛是心腸惡毒的美女讓馬克很驚訝。

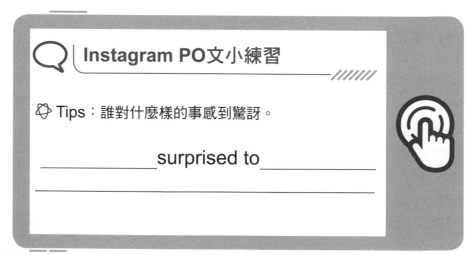

Instagram PO文小練習

Tips：誰對什麼樣的事感到驚訝。

_____ surprised to _____

_____

作文範例

Often we hear the claim that any child can be taught to be a good sports person or musicians. Even if some of those traits can be taught, we do have other things to consider. Is it possible for a 5'4 basketball player, even if he or she is well-trained, to be able to compete with a person who is 6'4 or will the 5'4 basketball player be chosen by NBA? Do you think that we can be a great musician or sports person simply through determination and teaching?

1 The claim that any child can be taught to become a good sports person or musicians is entirely incorrect. Our hereditary traits already determine who we are when we are born. Teaching plays a minor role in talent-related fields, such as sports or music.

2 Our height, for example, is largely determined by gene of our parents. There is no other ways for a 5'4 basketball player, even if he or she is well-trained, to compete with a person who is 6'4.

3 Furthermore, the chance for that person to be trained and chosen to be an NBA player is infinitesimal. The claim here may be harsh, but it is just the reality. Also, most well-known players are genetically gifted in certain areas with a particular emphasis on hard work and perseverance.

4 Indeed, there are rare examples of certain people who are successful in certain fields because of their perseverance and endurance. It cannot be justified the fact that how important it is to have genetically natural abilities to excel in certain areas. Moreover, the statement of whether it is a waste of not using the talent is not in the discussion of the topic.

5 In conclusion, some talents are inborn. It is surprise to find a statement that says we can be trained to be Mozart. We cannot be Mozart simply through hard work, perseverance, and teaching. Teaching will only assist us to reach to a certain goal, but it will not outweigh the effects inborn talents have on us. Therefore, we cannot be taught to be a good sports or well-known musicians.

作文中譯加解析

　　通常我們聽到這個陳述，任何小孩能透過教導而成為良好的運動員或音樂家。即使有些特質能透過教導，我們有其他事可以考慮。對於一個身高五呎四吋的籃球選手，即使受過良好訓練是有可能與六呎四吋的籃球選手競爭嗎？又或者是身高五呎四吋的籃球選手會為 NBA 選拔中雀屏中選嗎？你認為一個偉大的音樂家或運動員能只靠決心和教學嗎？

1 主張任何小孩能被教導成良好的運動員或音樂家是完全不正確的。我們的遺傳特質已經於我們出生決定了我們是誰。教導在才能相關的領域，像是運動或音樂上，扮演著較輕微的角色。

　• 首段定義小孩能被教導成良好的運動員或音樂家是完全不正確的。畢竟遺傳因素很大程度地決定我們的發展。

2 例如我們的身高，由我們父母的基因大幅地決定了。對於一個五呎四吋高的籃球選手，即使他或她受過良好訓練，能與一個六呎四吋的選手競爭，是不可能的。

　• 第二段以身高舉例一個五呎四吋高的籃球選手，即使他或她受過良好訓練，能與一個六呎四吋的選手競爭，是不可能的。

3 此外，對於那個人來說，能被 NBA 選中且訓練的機會是微乎其微的。這個主張可能嚴屬，但這就是現實。而且，大多數知名的運動員都是在特定領域上具遺傳上的天賦，尤其在努力和毅力上輔以特

189

別的強化。

- 第三段說明現實因素,並說明大多數知名的運動員都是在特定領域上具遺傳上的天賦,尤其在努力和毅力上輔以特別的強化。

4 的確,有罕見的例子,有特定的人在特別領域上很成功因為她們的毅力和耐力。但卻無法合理的證明具有遺傳上的天賦,而擅長在特定領域上的發展多麼重要的。此外,這個陳述不論是否沒使用這項天賦而是浪費的,這也不在這個話題的討論範圍。

- 第三段說明的確有罕見的例子,有特定的人在特別領域上很成功因為她們的毅力和耐力。但是遺傳上的天賦仍決定了擅長在特定領域上的發展多麼重要的。

5 結論是,有些天賦是與生俱來的。令人感到驚訝的是,我們發現有受訓練就能成為莫札特的陳述。我們不可能成為莫札特僅透過努力毅力和教學。教學只會協助我們達到某個特定的目標,但是確無法蓋過與生俱來的天賦對我們造成的影響。因此,我們不可能成為良好的運動員或知名的音樂家。

- 最後說明有些天賦是與生俱來的。教學只會協助我們達到某個特定的目標,但是確無法蓋過與生俱來的天賦對我們造成的影響。並以莫札特為例。

字彙補一補

1. hereditary **adj.** 遺傳的
Everyone has a different hereditary trait.
每個人有不同的遺傳特徵。

2. determine **v.** 決定
Our life is not entirely determined by the surroundings.
我們的生活不全然由環境決定。

3. infinitesimal **adj.** 微乎其微的
The winning chance is infinitesimal.
贏出的機會是微乎其微的。

4. rare **adj.** 罕見的
Coming down with the flu under this kind of weather is rare.
在這種天氣下患感冒是很罕見的。

5. endurance **n.** 耐力
Walking in the desert requires endurance.
在沙漠中行走需要耐力。

6. discussion **n.** 討論
The discussion is like forever.
討論像是沒完沒了。

重點解析

1. There is no other ways for a 5'4 basketball player, even if he or she is well-trained, to compete with a person who is 6'4.

   對於一個五呎四吋高的籃球選手，即使他或她受過良好訓練，能與一個六呎四吋的選手競爭，是不可能的。

   - a 5'4 basketball player 表示五呎四吋高的籃球選手。
   - There is/there are 為常用的基本句型，其句型後常接代名詞或名詞，再加上時間或地點，There is no other ways 表示是不可能的，沒有其他方法。
   - well-trained 表示訓練有素。
   - compete with 表示與…競爭。
   - who 引導關係代名詞子句，句中為 a person who is 6'4 表示六呎四吋的人。

2. Furthermore, the chance for that person to be trained and chosen to be an NBA player is infinitesimal.

   此外，對於那個人來說，能被NBA選中且訓練的機會是微乎其微的。

   - furthermore 表示此外…。
   - the chance for that person to be trained and chosen to be an NBA player 表示對於那個人來說，能被 NBA 選中且訓練的機會。
   - infinitesimal 表示微乎其微的。

3. Also, most well-known players are genetically gifted in certain areas with a particular emphasis on hard work and perseverance.

> • also 表示而且為承轉詞。
> • most well-known players 表示大多數之名的選手。
> • genetically gifted in certain areas 表示在特定領域中具遺傳上地天賦。
> • with a particular emphasis 表示特別加強…。

Unit 19

intend to
想要

 可以這樣寫 ////////////

1. He intends to get rid of his potbelly.
   他想要除掉他的游泳圈。

2. He intends to write a travel book in two weeks.
   他想要在兩週內寫本旅遊書。

句型小貼士 ....

- 不定詞用法很廣，其中具有名詞、形容詞和副詞的功用。不定詞作為受詞的動詞很多有 intend、ask、expect、mean、plan、offer 等等。不定詞作為受詞的句型為 S+V+to V。

- potbelly 表示大肚子，引申為游泳圈，為極常見的用法。

句型腦激盪

★He intends to get rid of the birthmark.
⇨He intends to get rid of the hideous birthmark.
他想要除掉醜陋的胎記。

★He intends to get rid of a potbelly.
⇨He intends to get rid of a greasy potbelly.
他想要除掉油膩的游泳圈。

★He intends to get rid of a fat ass.
⇨He intends to get rid of a fat ass by taking exercise four times a week.
他想藉由 1 週 4 次的運動來除掉肥滋滋的屁股。

★He intends to get rid of a dark skin.
⇨He intends to get rid of a dark skin with a lot of freckles.
他想要擺脫長了一大堆雀斑的暗沈皮膚。

★He intends to get rid of a pimple.
⇨He intends to get rid of a bad-looking pimple.
他想要除掉不好看的青春痘。

★He intends to get rid of metabolism problems.
⇨He intends to get rid of unsolved metabolism problems.
他想要除掉未解決的代謝問題。

★He intends to get rid of drinking problems.
⇨He intends to get rid of frequent drinking problems.
他想要除掉頻繁的酗酒問題。

★He intends to get rid of a 22K.
⇨ He intends to get rid of a disappointing 22K.
他想要擺脫掉令人失望的 22K 薪資。

★He intends to get rid of his thin legs.
⇨ He intends to get rid of his thin legs with lots of hair.
他想要擺脫掉他瘦不拉嘰的毛毛腿。

★He intends to get rid of a landlord.
⇨ He intends to get rid of an annoying landlord.
他想要擺脫煩人的房東。

Instagram PO文小練習

Tips：你最想要擺脫什麼呢？

I intend to _____
_____

作文範例

Studies have shown that at an early age, children are more apt to learn a foreign language because their thinking pattern is more flexible, but others have a different opinion, fearing that children learning a foreign language at an early age will have a negative influence on their mother tongue. What is your opinion?

1 Ages at which kids begin to learn a foreign language have been debated. However, there is a concern for most of us even if we are not teachers or parents. Which is really the best for our future generations?

2 Studies have been shown that at an early age children are more apt to learn a foreign language because their thinking pattern is more flexible, but most adults, while intending to emulate foreign accents and grammatical rules are struggling to find a way out. They are starting to learn both languages. It is good. Unlike most adults or high school students, who are thinking in Chinese mostly, kids encounter fewer obstacles to learn a foreign language. Their thinking is not fixated. Kids seldom produce Chinglish. They are not influenced by Chinese. They are better speakers. They are not afraid of saying English in front of the public.

3 Furthermore, it might seem surprising to most of us, but studies have shown that primary school students have a better listening score than high school students. They are attentive while listening to English. These are all the advantages for primary school students. They are like a plastic, but they have not been molded. They are versatile. The flexibility has enabled them to learn a foreign language. They should not wait until they have been molded. They should seize the golden period to learn a foreign language.

4 To sum up, from the above-mentioned statements, I do think it is better for primary school students to start learning a foreign language, and get rid of this annoying problem and wondering whether our kids should learn a foreign language at an early age or not.

作文中譯加解析

研究顯示小孩在初期更易於學習外語，因為他們的思考模式更具彈性，但是其他人有著不同的看法，擔心小孩於早期學習外語會對本身母語有負面的影響。你的看法是？

1 小孩開始學習外語的年紀一直備受爭議。然而，對於我們大多數的人來說，即使我們不是老師或父母，還是個擔憂。但是對於我們下一代什麼才是最佳的呢？

• 首段先定義小孩開始學習外語的年紀一直備受爭議。而這確實讓人擔憂，最後提出反問，到底對於我們下一代什麼才是最佳的呢？

2 研究顯示小孩在初期更易於學習外語，因為他們的思考模式更具彈性。他們正開始學習兩種語言。這樣是好的。不像大多數以中文思考的成年人或高中學生，小孩在學習外語的時候，遭受到較少的障礙。他們的思考模式不是固定的。但大多數的成年人在想要模仿外國口音及文法規時卻往往是不得其門而入。小孩較少產生中式英文。他們沒有受到中文的影響。他們是較好的口說者。他們不擔心在大眾面前講英文。

• 第二段說明研究顯示小孩在初期更易於學習外語，因為他們的思考模式更具彈性。說明這個時期學習外語的優點，由其在思維方面和口說上。

3 此外，對我們大多數的人來說似乎可能感到驚訝，但研究顯示小孩比高中學生有較好的聽力成績。他們在聽英文的時候更專注。這些對於國小學生來說都是優點。他們就像是塑膠但是卻未被定型。他們是很多樣的。具彈性已使得他們能夠學習外語。他們不該等到已被定型後。他們應該抓住黃金時期學習外語。

• 第三段說明研究顯示小孩比高中學生有較好的聽力成績。他們在聽英文的時候更專注。並以塑膠為例來形容他們學習上的優勢，他們不會被定型，能在黃金時期學外語。

4 總之，從以上陳述，我認為優點是多於缺點的。對小學生來說開始學習外語是較好的，擺脫這個擾人的問題然後想著我們的小孩是否該於成長初期學習外語。

• 最後總結出對對小學生來說開始學習外語是較好的。

字彙補一補

1. pattern **n.** 模式

Her thinking pattern is very unique.

她的思考模式非常的獨特。

2. flexible **adj.** 具彈性的

This job requires a person who is more flexible and open.

這份工作需要更具彈性且開放的人。

3. obstacles **n.** 障礙

Even though we encounter obstacles every now and then, we are still very optimistic.

即使我們偶爾面臨障礙，我們仍非常的樂觀。

4. influence **n.** 影響

The Internet has a huge influence on our lives.

網路對我們生活有巨大的影響。

5. surprising **adj.** 令人感到驚訝的

The result is quite surprising.

結果令人感到相當驚訝。

6. seize **v.** 抓住⋯機會

When an opportunity presents itself, we need to seize opportunities.

當機會出現時，我們需要抓住機會。

| 重點解析

1. Studies have been shown that at an early age children are more apt to learn a foreign language because their thinking pattern is more flexible.

研究顯示小孩在初期更易於學習外語，因為他們的思考模式更具彈性。

- Studies have been shown that 表示研究已顯示…，於學術文章中常見。
- are more apt to 表示更易於…。
- because 引導副詞子句，其句型為 S+V …becauseS+V。
- thinking pattern 表示思考模式。

2. Unlike most adults or high school students, who are thinking in Chinese mostly, kids encounter fewer obstacles to learn a foreign language.

不像大多數以中文思考的成年人或高中學生，小孩在學習外語的時後，遭受到較少的障礙。

- unlike 為介詞，其句型為 unlike+介詞片語，S+V(主要子句)。
- who 引導關係代名詞子句，句中為 who are thinking in Chinese mostly 表示大部分以中文思考。
- encounter fewer obstacles 表示遭遇到較少的障礙。

3. Furthermore, it might seem surprising to most of us, but studies have shown that there primary school students have a better listening score than high school students.

此外，對我們大多數的人來說似乎可能感到驚訝，但研究顯示小孩比高中學生有較好的聽力成績。

- furthermore 表示此外為承轉詞。
- it might seem surprising to most of us 表示對我們大多數的人來說似乎可能感到驚訝。
- studies have shown 表示研究已顯示…。
- have a better listening score than high school students. 表示小孩比高中學生有較好的聽力成績。

20 notice
注意到

 可以這樣寫

/////////

1. The opponent has noticed his Achilles heel.
   敵手已注意到他的致命缺點。

2. The basketball player has noticed his teammate's Achilles heel is dragging down the entire team.
   籃球手已經注意到他隊友的致命缺點正拖垮整個團隊。

句型小貼士

• 感官動詞用法很廣，其後加受詞再加上原形動詞/Ving 或 p.p。

• 感官動詞包含了 see, watch, look at, hear, listen to, feel, notice 等等。

• Achilles heel 用於形容一個人的致命缺點，由神話中衍生的，為極常見的用法。

⚡ 句型腦激盪

★The designer has noticed she has a birthmark.

⇨The designer has noticed she has a hideous birthmark.

設計師已注意到她有醜陋的胎記。

★He has noticed his client has a potbelly.

⇨He has noticed his client has a greasy potbelly.

他已注意到他的客戶有肥滋滋的游泳圈。

★The husband has noticed his wife has a fat ass.

⇨The husband has noticed his lovely wife has a fat ass.

丈夫已注意到他的親愛的妻子有肥胖的屁股。

★The opponent has noticed he has an unchanged attitude.

⇨The opponent has noticed lately he has an unchanged attitude.

敵手最近已注意到他有著不改變的態度。

★The shop owner has noticed the kid is curious about everything.

⇨The shop owner has noticed the kid is extensively curious about everything.

店主已注意到這小孩對於所有事都感到十分地好奇。

★The matchmaker has noticed he has a pleasing appearance.

⇨The matchmaker has noticed immediately he has a pleasing appearance.

媒婆立即就注意到他有著討人喜歡的外貌。

★The interviewer has noticed the interviewee a reserved countenance.

⇨The interviewer has noticed the young interviewee a reserved countenance.

面試官已注意到這一個年輕的面試者有著含蓄的面容。

★The teacher has noticed he has a brilliant mind.

⇨The teacher has noticed he has a brilliant mind which does not match his age.

老師已注意到他有著出色的頭腦。

★The boss has noticed his staff.

⇨The boss has noticed a great passion in his staff.

老闆已注意到他的職員的極大熱情。

★Jane's mother has noticed her motivation.

⇨Jane's mother has noticed her unkind motivation.

珍的母親已注意到她不善的動機。

Instagram PO文小練習

Tips：你注意到了什麼呢？

I have noticed _____

_____

作文範例

Job satisfaction is perhaps the most important thing in the workplace. Moreover, it is unlikely for most of us to find the job we 100% like. There are certainly lots of things that we can find fault with that we are unhappy about. What is your opinion?

1 Since the vast majority of people spend their time at work, at least a minimum of 8 hours per working day, the satisfaction of job is an important factor for people to stay at a company.

2 It is important for people to feel satisfied with their job since they have to spend most of their time working there. Even if job satisfaction is related to many areas, ranging from salaries, job content, relevance of one's expertise, colleagues, executives, and so on, people can still find ways to feel good about themselves. We notice that not all things are perfect after all. Some people work in a prestigious company, but they are always under tight deadline. Sometimes they are faced with incoming calls all day long. While others are working near their lovely home, they have a low-paid job.

3 Positivity is the key to your job because there is always something you do not like in your jobs, and there is always something you love about it when you walk in the office. Stop making comparison with others. Things will get so much easier if we do not think it too much.

4 To sum up, all the above mentioned factors have affected well-being of individuals in the workplace. People tend to have a different opinion on what is important and what is not. Some value certain factors more. Others rank particular factors on the list of the job satisfaction survey, if we have a positive mindset, we will see things differently, feeling everything around us is so great that we do not have to worry about things we do not have.

作文中譯加解析

　　工作滿意度可能是在職場中最重要的事。此外，對我們大多數的人來說我們不太可能找到我們百分之百滿意的工作。也確實有太多我們可以挑剔或我們不高興的部分。你的看法是？

1 既然大多數的人花費時間工作，每個工作天至少 8 小時，工作滿意度對留住人來說是很重要的因素。

- 首段指出人們所花費在工作上的時間，所以工作滿意度對人們來說是很重要的因素。

2 對人們來說對滿意自己從事的工作是很重要的，既然他們要花費大多數的時間在那工作。即使工作滿意度與許多領域有所關聯，從薪資、工作內容、每個人專業能力的相關性、同事、主管等等，人們仍可以找到讓他們感覺良好的部分。並非所有事情都是完美的。有些人在享譽盛名的公司工作，但他們卻總是戰戰兢兢。他們可能每天都不斷面臨電話打進來，而其他人可能在離溫暖的家很近的地方工作，卻有著低薪的工作。

- 第二段說明要人們花費大多數的時間在那工作。雖然影響工作滿意度的因素很多，對人們來說能滿意自己從事的工作是很重要的，最後指出事情不可能都照我們想的走，找到錢多事少離家近的工作。

3 正向思考對工作來說是關鍵,因為當你走進公司時,工作中總是有些事是你不喜歡的,而且總是有些　你喜愛的。停止於其他人比較。事情會變的很輕鬆,如果我們不過度思考。

- 第三段説明正向思考的重要性,畢竟工作中總是有些事是你不喜歡的,而且總是有些是你喜愛的。停止於其他人比較。事情會變的很輕鬆。

4 總之,以上所有的因素已經影響到每個人在職場中的幸福感。人們傾向對哪些事重要的,而哪些不是有不同的意見。有些人更重視特定的因素。其他人則把特定因素列在工作滿意度調查的清單上。如果我們都抱持著正向的態度,我們看事情的角度也會不同,感受到我們周遭的事情都很棒,以至於我們不用擔心我們不該擔心的。

- 最後表明很多因素已經影響到每個人在職場中的幸福感。不管影響每個人的工作滿意度的因素為何,有正向態度都能使自己滿意自己的工作。

字彙補一補

1. vast **adj.** 廣大的
   There is a vast room for us to enjoy.
   有著廣大的房間供我們享受。

2. minimum **n.** 最低限度
   People have to spend at least the minimum of 150 dollars in this coffee shop.
   在這間咖啡店裡，人們至少要花費最低限度 150 元。

3. satisfaction **n.** 滿意
   Job satisfaction is related to the time employees will work in a specific company.
   工作滿意度與員工們在一家特定公司裡工作的時間有關。

4. relevance **n.** 相關性
   When you are considering changing a job, the relevance between the current job and the next job is very important.
   當你考慮換工作時，現在工作和下份工作的相關性是非常重要的。

5. perfect **adj.** 完美的
   Looking for the perfect person is unrealistic.
   尋找一個完美的人是不切實際的。

6. prestigious **adj.** 享譽盛名的
   Oxford is a prestigious university.
   牛津是所享譽盛名的大學。

重點解析 ////////

1. Even if job satisfaction is related to many areas, ranging from salaries, job content, relevance of one's expertise, colleagues, executives, and so on, people can still find ways to feel good about themselves.

即使工作滿意度與許多領域有所關聯，從薪資、工作內容、每個人專業能力的相關性、同事、主管等等，人們仍可以找到讓他們感覺良好的部分。

- Even if 表示即使…，引導副詞子句，其句型為 Even if+S+V，S+V(主要子句)，people can still find ways to feel good about themselves 為主要子句。
- be related to 表示與…相關。
- range from A to B 表示從 A 到 B。
- and so on 表示等等…。
- can still find ways to feel good about themselves 仍可以找到讓他們感覺良好的部分。

2. Positivity is the key to your job because there is always something you do not like in your jobs, and there is always something you love about it when you walk in the office.

正向思考對工作來説是關鍵，因為當你走進公司時，工作中總是有些事是你不喜歡的，而且總是有些是你喜愛的。

- the key to 表示是…關鍵。
- because 表示因為…，引導副詞子句，其句型為 because+S+V，S+V（主要子句），Positivity is the key to your job 為主要子句。

- There is/there are 為常用的基本句型，其句型後常接代名詞或名詞，再加上時間或地點。
- when 表示時間…，引導副詞子句，其句型為 when+S+V，S+V（主要子句），there is always something you love about it 為主要子句。

3. While others are working near their lovely home, they have a low-paid job.

而其他人可能在離溫暖的家很近的地方工作，卻有著低薪的工作。

- while 表示儘管…，引導副詞子句，其句型為 while+S+V，S+V（主要子句），they have a low-paid job 為主要子句。
- are working near their lovely home 表示在他們溫馨的家附近工作。
- a low-paid job 表示低薪工作。

it has become
這已經成了

可以這樣寫

1. It has become elephant in the room.
   這已經成了大家不想碰觸的事實。

2. It seems that it has become an inermational health issue.
   這似乎已經成了國際性的健康議題。

句型小貼士

- 連綴動詞用法很廣,為不完全不及物動詞,後面加主詞補語。

- 連綴動詞包含了 seem, remain, appear, sound, look, become 等等。

- Elephant in the room 意指為問題很大,但大家都視若無睹不去處理,為極常見的用法。

⚡ 句型腦激盪

★It has become a huge problem.
⇨It has become a huge problem that no one wants to get involved.
　這已經成了大家不想被牽涉到的大問題。

★It has become an issue.
⇨It has become an unsolved issue.
　這已經成了未解決的議題。

★It has become an opportunity.
⇨It has become a great opportunity.
　這已經成了極佳的機會。

★It has become a quarrel.
⇨It has become a quarrel with trivial matters.
　這已經成了為瑣事而爭吵。

★It has become a fight.
⇨It has become a fight for life.
　這已經成了為生存而戰。

★It has become a struggle.
⇨It has become a continuing struggle.
　這已經成了持續的掙扎。

★It has become a dilemma.
⇨It has become an unresolved dilemma.
　這已經成了沒有解決的難題。

★It has become compensation.
⇨It has become huge compensation.
這已經成了極大的補償。

★It has become a difficult situation.
⇨It has become a difficult situation that I really don't know what to do.
這已經成了我真的不知怎樣解決的困難處境。

★It has become an unexpected turn.
⇨It has become an unexpected turn in his life.
這已經成在他生命中意料之外的改變。

Instagram PO文小練習

✧ Tips：在這個句子中的 become 接在 has 後面為過去分詞，代表的是現在完成式。

It has become _____

_____

作文範例

The function of the university has been debated. Bosses and executives are complaining that graduates are far less likely to perform the job they request. They think courses taken by graduates during four years of college are not useful to an employer, but others tend to think courses should be designed to acquire knowledge, not strictly confined to practicality and usefulness. What is your opinion?

1 Whether universities should provide students with adequate knowledge and skills required in the workplace has long been debated. In real life, it really matters from subjects to subjects.

2 There have always been complaints from bosses and executives that graduates are far less likely to perform to the job they are requested. There is a gap between school teaching and workplace. Most of the time, some subjects are theory-based. Most graduates seem to have a hard time getting accustomed to the workplace once they are hired. Most of the statements are probably true or might as well be true when those executives fill in the questionnaires. It takes more time to assist those graduates to adapt in the work-place.

3 All these statements have led us to rethink about school programs. Everyone spends so much time and money to be in the university, hoping that they can eventually find a decent job. In real life, this has not been the case. A lot of students graduating from colleges or universities doing the job that is nothing like their own majors. Most of them complain that all school courses are not helping. They wish their universities could teach them necessary skills that will be utilized in the workplace. Schools should not be teaching whatever they think is right for students. Furthermore, most professors do not real working experiences.

4 To sum up, from above-mentioned statements, we do not want to become a jobless person, and there is certainly a need for schools to teach knowledge and skills needed in the workplace. After all, finding the truth in philosophy and many things will only get you into nowhere, struggling to one job after another.

作文中譯加解析

Unit 15
Unit 16
Unit 17
Unit 18
Unit 19
Unit 20
Unit 21
Unit 22
Unit 23
Unit 24
Unit 25
Unit 26
Unit 27
Unit 28

　　大學的功能一直備受爭論。老闆們和主管們抱怨著，畢業生在執行工作上遠達不到他們所要求的。他們認為畢業生四年大學期間所修的課對雇主來說是沒有用的，但是其他人傾向於認為課程設計上應該是獲取知識，而非僅僅是侷限於實用性和有用。你的看法是？

1 大學是否應該提供學生在職場所需的足夠知識和技能一直備受爭議。在現實生活中，這真的因為學科的不同而不同。

- 首段先定義出大學是否應該提供學生在職場所需的足夠知識和技能一直備受爭議。而這也的確會因為學科的不同而需要的知識和技能也不同。

2 老闆們和主管們一直對於畢業生在執行工作上遠達不到他們所要求的有所抱怨。在學校教學和職場是存在差距的。大多數的時候，有些學科是以理論為基礎的。大多數的畢業生，一但被雇用後，的確很難適應職場。大多數的陳述可能是真的或很可能是真的當那些主管填了問卷後。是需要更多的時間去協助那些畢業生適應職場的。

- 第二段說明老闆和主管們的看法，也指出學校教學和職場實際上的落差，另一方面也說明有些學科是以理論為基礎的。而的確大多數的畢業生需要時間去適應職場，而且是需要主管協助的。

3 所有的這些陳述已使得我們重新思考學校的課程。每個人花費很多時間跟金錢上大學，期許他們最終能夠找到不錯的工作。在現實生活中，事實卻非如此。很多學生從學院或大學畢業後，卻從事與自己專業不同的工作。他們大多數抱怨學校課程沒有助益。他們希望他們的大學能夠教他們於職場上必須的技能。學校不該教導他們認為對學生是有助益的。此外，大多數的教授並沒有實際工作經驗。

- 第三段提出反思，所有的這些陳述已使得我們重新思考學校的課程。畢竟每個人花費很多時間跟金錢上大學，期許他們最終能夠找到不錯的工作。另一方面也指出學生實際需求，他們希望他們的大學能夠教他們於職場上必須的技能。學校不該教導他們認為對學生是有助益的。

4 總之，從以上陳述，我們不想成為失業的人，而學校確實有需要教導職場上所需要技能。畢竟，在哲學中找尋真理和許多事並不會引領到對的地方，只會讓你在找工作時接續掙扎著。

- 最後表明自己的看法說明學校確實有需要教導職場上所需要技能。

字彙補一補

1. complaint **n.** 抱怨
Complaints from customers are going to affect her year-end bonuses.
顧客的抱怨將影響到她年終獎金。

2. perform **n.** 執行
Knowing how to perform the task is very important.
懂得如何執行任務是非常重要的。

3. theory-based **adj.** 已理論為基礎的
Theory-based courses can also be interesting.
以理論為基礎的課也可以很有趣。

4. accustomed **adj.** 適應的
He is accustomed to the marine environment.
他適應了海洋環境。

5. statement **n.** 陳述
His statement in front of judges weighs heavily on whether the accused will be convicted or not.
他在法官面前的陳述將大幅的影響到被告是否會被定罪。

6. eventually **adv.** 最後地
He will eventually get what he wants.
他最終會得到他想要的。

| 重點解析

1. There have always been complaints from bosses and executives that graduates are far less likely to perform to the job they are requested.

老闆們和主管們一直對於畢業生在執行工作上遠達不到他們所要求的有所抱怨。

- are far less likely to 表示較不可能。
- perform to the job they are requested 表示執行他們被要求的工作。

2. Most of the statements are probably true or might as well be true when those executives fill in the questionnaires.

大多數的陳述可能是真的或很可能是真的當那些主管填了問卷後。

- probably true 可能是真的。
- might as well be true 也可能是真的。
- fill in the questionnaires 表示填問卷。
- when 表示時間…，引導副詞子句，其句型為 when+S+V，S+V（主要子句），Most of the statements are probably true or might as well be true 為主要子句。

3. They wish their universities could teach them necessary skills that will be utilized in the workplace.

他們希望他們的大學能夠教他們於職場上必須的技能。

- teach them necessary skills 表示教導必須的技能。
- that 引導關係代名詞子句，句中為 that will be utilized in the workplace 表示能於職場中用到的，修飾技能。

Unit 22

both A and B
A 與 B 兩者都…

可以這樣寫

//////////

1. Both John and I know that there is casting couch for certain jobs.

   約翰和我都知道對特定工作來說是有檯面下的潛規則。

2. The casting couch for certain jobs is both unethical and obscene.

   特定工作的檯面下的潛規則是不道德且猥褻的。

句型小貼士

....

- both A and B…表示 A 與 B 兩者都,為常見句型,須注意其後加複數動詞。

- both A and B…為連接詞片語連接兩主詞題型,相關用法還有 either or, neither nor, not only but also 等等。

- casting couch …指檯面下的潛規則,通常與性有關,為極常見的用法。

句型腦激盪

★Both John and I know that it is adopted in our country.

⇨Both John and I know that it is widely adopted in our country.

約翰和我都知道在我們的國家這是廣泛被採用的。

★Both Lisa and I know that the use of the company jet is confined to the boss.

⇨Both Lisa and I know that the use of the company jet is strictly confined to the boss.

莉莎和我都知道公司噴射機僅限於老闆使用。

★Both Jessica and I know that tonight drinking alcohol will not be regulated.

⇨Both Jessica and I know that tonight drinking alcohol will not be regulated by the company policies.

潔西卡和我都知道今晚飲酒不受公司規定的規範。

★Both John and I know that driving speed is not restricted.

⇨Both John and I know that in some places, driving speed is not restricted.

約翰和我都知道在有些地方行駛速度是不受限制的。

★Both John and I know that office stationary has been abused.

⇨Both John and I know that office stationary has been always abused.

約翰和我都知道公司文具已被濫用。

★Both Mary and I know that Harry Potter series are fictions.

⇨Both Mary and I know that Harry Potter series are well-known fictions.

瑪莉和我都知道對哈利波特系列是知名的小說。

★Both John and I know that that haunted house.
⇨Both John and I know that that haunted house is little-known.

約翰和我都知道那間鬼屋是鮮為人知的。

★Both Jack and I know that it is not a promotion notification.
⇨Both Jack and I know that it is not an official promotion notification.

傑克和我都知道這還不算是正式的升遷通知。

Instagram PO文小練習

🌐 Tips：你和誰之間共同分享著的秘密是？

_____and I know that_____

_____

作文範例

There is an unspoken rule that people in certain professions, such as sports professionals earn big bucks, while others pale in comparison. What is your opinion?

1 Successful sports professionals earning a great deal of money than people in other important professions are widely-understood, and on the surface, it may seem fair that they deserve to get paid based on their hard work and contribution to the athlete world, but a close look reveals the fact that there are other reasons that need to be considered.

2 With bucks of money bringing in for most companies, ranging from advertising, fashion, athletic-related fields, sports athletes have become an icon for younger generations. Even though some of them have to undergo a rigorous training, most people think they are resting on their own luck. Therefore, it has created an image that they do not have to work hard than people in other important professions. Furthermore, some of them are the spokesmen or spokeswomen, but they actually set a bad example for most people who emulate them.

3 Also, in rare cases, they do become successful without hard work. They are in a route not normal people would follow. Most people still have to study and go to university. For most people, they are the exceptions, not the rules. Thus, most people think it is unreasonable for them to earn more money than people in other important professions. Their income should be restricted. More should be stressed that people should get a good education, get the fruits of success through hard work, and be in an industry undergone a rigorous training for a long time.

4 For all these reasons, I do think the income of most athletes should be restricted even though they get paid based on both of their hard work and contribution to the athlete world. Therefore, it is not fully justified to say that they should earn more than other important professions.

作文中譯加解析

人們所從事的特定行業，例如運動專業人員，有著不成文規定，即是他們賺進大把鈔票，而其它的人卻相形見絀。你的想法是？

1 成功的體育專業人員比從事其它重要行業的人賺很多錢是廣為人知的。表面上，他們是基於他們的努力和對運動界的貢獻，而應得到這些報酬，這看似合理的，但是仔細檢視之下，揭露了是有其他理由是需要考慮進去的。

- 首段先定義成功的體育專業人員比從事其它重要行業的人賺很多錢是廣為人知的。以致於許多人會覺得是理所當然的。

2 隨著大多數公司，從廣告、流行、運動相關的領域，賺進大把鈔票，體育運動家已成為年輕世代的偶像。即使他們有些人必須經歷嚴格的訓練，而大多數的人卻認為他們純粹是單憑運氣。因此，這產生了一個印象，就是他們不用像其它重要行業的人一樣很努力。此外，他們有些人是男代言人或女代言人，但他們實際上對於大多數模仿他們的人樹立了壞榜樣。

- 第二段說明不管這些人是必須經歷嚴格的訓練，或純粹是單憑運氣。因此，這產生了一個印象，讓人們以為他們不用像其它重要行業的人一樣很努力。另一方面則是他們對青少年的影響，還成了模仿者的壞榜樣。

3 而且，在罕見的例子中，他們的確能成功卻不需要努力。他們走的道路不是一般人所走的。大多數的人仍然必須學習和上大學。對大多數的人而言，他們是例外，而非常態。因此，大多數的人認為比從事其他重要行業的人來說，他們賺取更多錢是不合理的。他們的收入是該被限制的。更重要的是人們該受良好教育，透過努力而收穫成功的果實，在行業中經歷過長期嚴格的訓練。

• 第三段指出在罕見的例子中，他們的確能成功卻不需要努力。大多數的人認為比從事其他重要行業的人來說，他們賺取更多錢是不合理的。他們的收入是該被限制的。傳統價值觀使得大家認為人們是需要受良好教育，透過努力而收穫成功的果實。

4 總之，基於這些原因，我認為大多數運動員的收入應被限制，即使他們所得是基於他們的努力跟對運動業的貢獻。因此，對於他們應該賺比其它重要行業更多是不完全合理的。

• 最後提出自己的看法，這裡使用了 For all these reasons（基於這些原因）可被認為是重述法做為末段的總結，來表明大多數運動員的收入應被限制的。

字彙補一補

1. successful **adj.** 成功的
   To be a successful person is not hard.
   要成為一個成功人士不難。

2. athletic-related **adj.** 運動相關的
   Athletic-related fields are very interesting for most people.
   對大多數的人來說，運動相關的領域是非常有趣的。

3. undergo **v.** 經歷
   Undergoing a military training is not easy.
   經歷軍事訓練並不容易。

4. rigorous **adj.** 嚴格的
   We need to be rigorous towards this issue.
   我們要嚴肅的對待這一個議題。

5. unreasonable **adj.** 不合理的
   It is unreasonable for us for 12 hours a day.
   每日工作 12 小時是不合理的。

6. contribution **n.** 貢獻
   His contribution to museums is widely-known.
   他對博物館的貢獻是廣為人知的。

重點解析

1. Successful sports professionals earning a great deal of money than people in other important professions are widely-understood, and it is reasonable to make a comment that this should not be fully justified.

   成功的體育專業人員比從事其它重要行業的人賺很多錢是廣為人知的，而對此做出評論說這是不完全合理的是理所當然的。

   - who 引導關係代名詞子句，句中 earning 為 who earn 而來。
   - than 為表示程度的比較級…。
   - and 為對等連接詞連接兩句子。
   - it is reasonable to make a comment that…表示做此評論是合理的。

2. Even though some of them have to undergo a rigorous training, most people think they are resting on their own luck.

   即使他們有些人必須經歷嚴格的訓練，而大多數的人卻認為他們純粹是單憑運氣。

   - Even though 表語氣轉折…，引導副詞子句，其句型為 Even though+S+V，S+V（主要子句），most people think they are resting on their own luck 為主要子句。
   - undergo a rigorous training 表示經歷嚴格的訓練。
   - resting on their own luck 仰賴他們本身的運氣。

3. More should be stressed that people should get a good education, get the fruits of success through hard work, and be in an industry undergone a rigorous training for a long time.

更重要的是人們該受良好教育，透過努力而收穫成功的果實，在行業中經歷過長期嚴格的訓練。

> • More should be stressed that 表示應該更強調…。
> • the fruits of success 表示成功的果實。
> • through hard work 表示透過努力工作…。

have/has been regarded
被視為是

可以這樣寫

////////////

1. John has been regarded as a rotten apple.
   約翰一直都被視為是老鼠屎。

2. A rotten apple has been regarded an expression that is frequently used by Chinese.
   老鼠屎是中國人常用的用語。

句型小貼士

- regard A as B…為常見句型，只把 A 視為 B。

- 與 Regard A as B 同且指把 A 視為 B 的還有 think of，see, view, take 等等。

- a rotten apple 字面上意思是老鼠屎，個人不良的行為影響到大家，中文俗話常有一粒老鼠屎壞了一鍋粥的講法，為極常見的用法。

句型腦激盪

★John has been regarded as a rotten apple.

⇨ John has been regarded as a rotten apple with bad intention.

約翰一直都被視為是具不良意圖的老鼠屎。

★Jack has been regarded as an eye candy.

⇨ Jack has been regarded as an eye candy with no brain.

傑克一直都被視為是賞心悅目但無大腦的人。

★Having a fight with your spouse has been regarded as a bad influence.

⇨ Having a fight with your spouse has been regarded as a bad influence to kids.

與自己伴侶間的爭吵一直都被視為是對小孩子有不良的影響。

★Economic recession has been regarded as an impact.

⇨ Economic recession has been regarded as a huge impact.

經濟蕭條一直都被視為是具大的衝擊。

★Mary has been regarded as a potential buyer.

⇨ Mary has been regarded as a potential buyer with a great vision.

瑪莉一直都被視為是有遠見的潛力買家。

★Mark has been regarded as a well-to-do buyer.

⇨ Mark has been regarded as a well-to-do buyer who doesn't care about spending money.

馬克一直都被視為是不在乎花大錢的富有的買家。

★He has been regarded as a potential salesperson.

⇨He has been regarded by his boss as a potential salesperson.

他一直都被他的老闆視為是具潛力的銷售人員。

★Building a house on Mars has been regarded as a dream.

⇨Building a house on Mars has been regarded as a dream that will not come true.

在火星上建造房子一直都被視為是不可能實現的夢想。

★His proposal has been regarded as a great ambition.

⇨His proposal has been regarded as a great ambition in his working life.

他的提案一直都被視為是在他的職涯生活中的一個遠大的抱負。

★Killing your girlfriends has been regarded as an extreme act.

⇨Killing your girlfriends on the street has been regarded as an extreme act.

在街上砍殺你的女朋友一直都被視為是極端的行為。

Instagram PO文小練習

⚛ Tips：什麼事被認為是什麼呢？

_____has been regarded as_____

_____

作文範例

As a saying goes, while in Roman, do as the Romans do, but other people seem to have other opinions about whether people should follow local customs or not. Despite the fact that people understand access to certain regions is dangerous even with local residents' assistance, they get the access to those regions during their working holiday journey What is your opinion?

1 Whether visitors should conform to the norms of the local surroundings and behavior has been regarded as a debatable topic. The claim that the host country should welcome cultural differences is questionable also.

2 With the development of tourism, the question of whether visitors should conform to the norms of the local surroundings and behavior has arisen. Even with the preservation of the local culture and cultural landscape, the impact on the cultural traditions is inevitable.

3 Some of the visitors are arrogant and disrespectful; thus, making the value of cultural assets decline. They tend not to conform to the norms of the local custom. This behavior has resulted serious conflicts between local residents and visitors. There is always a reason why local residents act in a certain way and why other places are not allowed to be visited, but most visitors are too confident of themselves to conform to the norms. They challenge local customs. They visit certain places that they have been told not to. The next moment, they are facing the life and death.

4. Access to certain regions is largely dependent on local residents' understanding of the region. Some of the places are too dangerous to visit even with local residents' assistance. It is true that there is a reason why we should abide by the norms given by local people.

5. To sum up, for all these reasons from above, I think there are reasons why visitors should conform to the norms of the local surroundings and behavior, and we should obey them just as they are when they visit ours, we should not be so immature, getting access to dangerous regions during working holiday journey or traveling. With this understanding, local residents and visitors can get the respect from one another.

作文中譯加解析

　　俗話說得好，入境隨俗，但有人卻對人們是否遵守當地風俗有著不同的看法。儘管人們了解到達特定地區，即使有當地人的協助是危險的，他們在打工旅行的期間仍到那些地區。你的看法是？

1 拜訪者是否遵守當地環境的規範和行為一直備受爭論。主辦國家應該接受文化差異的宣稱也是受質疑的。

- 首段指出拜訪者是否遵守當地環境的規範和行為一直備受爭論。雙方文化的差異使得許多人都抱持的不同的看法。

2 隨著觀光業的發展，觀光客是否應該遵守當地環境的規範和行為的問題已經被提出。即使當地文化和文化景觀的保存，對文化傳統的衝擊是無可避免的。

- 第二段說明觀光客是否應該遵守當地環境的規範和行為會影響到對當地文化和文化景觀的保存和對文化傳統的衝擊。

3 有些觀光客是傲慢且不尊重人的；因此，使得文化資產的價值下降。他們傾向不遵守當地的習俗規範。這行為已經導致了當地居民和觀光客的嚴重衝突。當地居民會總是如何行事是有原因的，而且其他地方是禁止進入的，但是大多數的觀光客對於他們自己太過於自信以致於不遵守規範。他們挑戰當地習俗。他們拜訪了某些他們被告知是不可進入的地方。而下一刻，他們將會面臨生與死。

- 第三段說明不遵守當地的習俗規範的行為已經導致了當地居民和

Unit 15 / Unit 16 / Unit 17 / Unit 18 / Unit 19 / Unit 20 / Unit 21 / Unit 22 / Unit 23 / Unit 24 / Unit 25 / Unit 26 / Unit 27 / Unit 28

觀光客的嚴重衝突。傲慢且不尊重人的觀光客挑戰當地習俗使自己面臨生命危險。

4 到達特定的地區大多仰賴當地居民對於地區的了解。即使有當地居民的協助，進入有些地方還是太危險。這也是為什麼我們真的應該要遵守當地人所給的規範。

• 第四段說明之所以要遵守當地人所給的規範是有原因的。畢竟，到達特定的地區大多仰賴當地居民對於地區的了解。

5 總之，基於上述這些原因，我認為觀光客應該遵守當地習俗和行為是有理由的，且我們也應該遵守他們，就如同他們拜訪我們一樣。我們不該如此不成熟，在打工度假期間或旅行時，進入危險區域。有了這些體認，當地居民和觀光客能得到彼此的尊重。

• 最後表明自己的看法，遵守當地習俗和行為才能讓當地居民和觀光客能得到彼此的尊重。

字彙補一補

1. conform **v.** 遵守

   To conform to the norm is not easy.

   遵守規範不容易。

2. cultural **adj.** 文化的

   In this community, the cultural difference is huge.

   在這一個社區裡，文化差異很大。

3. questionable **adj.** 受質疑的

   Some acts are quite questionable.

   有些行為是相當受質疑的。

4. preservation **n.** 保存

   Preservation of the wild animals is very important.

   保護野生動物是非常重要的。

5. landscape **n.** 景色

   The landscape painting is beyond our imagination.

   這幅風景畫超出我們的想像。

6. conflict **n.** 衝突

   The conflict between subordinates and executives is serious.

   部屬和主管間的衝突是很嚴重的。

重點解析

1. With the development of tourism, the question of whether visitors should conform to the norms of the local surroundings and behavior has arisen.

隨著觀光業的發展，觀光客是否應該遵守當地環境的規範和行為的問題已經被提出。

- with 為介系詞，with the development of tourism 表示隨著觀光業的發展。
- with 的句型為 with+介詞片語，S+V（主要子句），the question of whether visitors should conform to the norms of the local surroundings and behavior has arisen 為主要子句。
- whether 表示是否…引導一名詞子句。
- conform to 遵守。

2. There is always a reason why local residents act in a certain way and why other places are not allowed to be visited, but most visitors are too confident of themselves to conform to the norms.

當地居民會總是如何行事是有原因的，而且其他地方是禁止進入的，但是大多數的觀光客對於它們自己太過於自信以致於不遵守規範。

- There is/there are 為常用的基本句型，其句型後常接代名詞或名詞，再加上時間或地點。
- and 為對等連接詞連接 why local residents act in a certain way and why other places are not allowed to be

visited 兩個子句。

- but 為對等連接詞表示語氣轉折。
- be confident of 表示對…有自信。

3. Some of the places are too dangerous to visit even with local residents' assistance.

即使有當地居民的協助，進入有些地方還是太危險

- too…to 表示太…而不能。
- even with 表示即使…有了。
- even with local residents' assistance 表示即使有了當地人的協助。

 可以這樣寫

1. To be an eye candy, one must have a great inheritance.

   要成為賞心悅目的俊男美女,要有良好的遺傳。

2. To be the cynosure at the party, one must be an eye candy.

   要成為舞會眾所矚目的焦點,要有賞心悅目的容貌。

句型小貼士

- 不定詞的使用用法極廣,在句中具有名詞、形容詞和副詞的功能,為常見句型,此句型為(To be…, S+V)。

- 不定詞當副詞用時,用以修飾形容詞或動詞,通常表示原因、理由等。

- an eye candy…字面上指視覺上具吸引注意力的人或物,意指賞心悅目的俊男美女。

⚡ 句型腦激盪

★To be a rotten apple, you have to be well-prepared.
⇨To be a rotten apple with bad intention, you have to be well-prepared.

要成為具不良意圖的老鼠屎，你必須準備充分。

★To be an eye candy, one must have a great inheritance.
⇨To be an eye candy, one must have a great inheritance from parents.

要成為賞心悅目的俊男美女，必需要得自父母親良好的遺傳。

★To be a successful businessman, you have to work very hard.
⇨To be a successful businessman, you have to work very hard.

要成為成功的商業人士，你必須非常努力。

★To be a accountant, you have to pay attention to details.
⇨To be a careful accountant, you have to pay attention to details.

要成為細心的會計，你必須注意細節。

★To be a great publisher, we must build up reputation.
⇨To be a great publisher, we must build up extremely good reputation.

要成為良好的出版商，我們必須建立極良好的聲譽。

★To be the arrogant cynosure, we do need to be overconfident.
⇨To be the arrogant cynosure for everyone, we do need to be overconfident.

要成為傲慢的眾人矚目焦點，我們需要過度的自信。

★To be a long-lasting company, we have to learn from success-ful examples.

⇨To be a long-lasting company, we have to learn from some successful examples.

要成為長期發展的公司，我們必須要從有些成功的例子中學習。

★To be a cotton empire, we have to beat other companies.

⇨To be a cotton empire, we have to beat many other rival com-panies.

要成為棉花帝國，我們必須要打敗許多其他競爭公司。

★To be a welcome guest, we have to be well-mannered.

⇨To be a welcome guest in the party, we have to be well-man-nered.

要成為這場派對上受歡迎的客人，我們要有良好的禮儀。

★To be an editor, we have to run many books.

⇨To be an outstanding editor, we have to run many books.

要成為傑出的編輯，我們要跑過許多書籍。

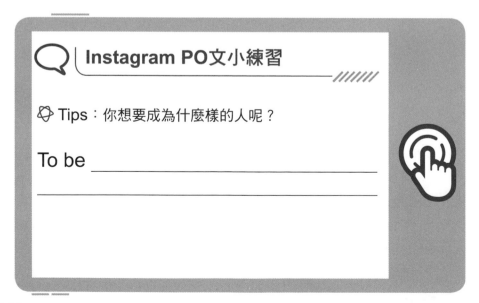

Instagram PO文小練習

Tips：你想要成為什麼樣的人呢？

To be _____

_____

作文範例

We have been encouraged to stay in the comfort zone and avoid changes, but we have to just dial back from the virtual world. After all, we encounter changes everyday, from our school days to our work. Changes are inevitable. What is your opinion? Is it true that changes are an inevitable process?

1 Most of us have been taught that reluctance to change is not good. It will only be a hindrance to our lives. Changes will make our life better.

2 In our life, it is true that we are going to encounter changes from our school days to our work. Whether we choose to remain the same or we choose to change, it is inevitable that we have to change in the long run. We have to adapt to the constantly-changing environment. To be a person who is reluctant to change is less likely to be a competitive person. There is no way that our environments adapt themselves to meet with our requirement.

3 In schools, there is no way that we pick every teacher from different subjects. We tell the school principal that we like certain art teacher better so that we should have an exchanged teacher scheme. In the workplace, there is no way that new executives change their management style to cater to us. Furthermore, even if you are the boss, there is no way that you constantly change your subordinates and executives. Of course, the boss totally has the right to do that, but that is not how usual companies run. Therefore, we have to encounter changes. We have to experience changes so that we can learn from those changes. A new executive, even though different from the previous one, can still have something extra, something worth-learning for us to learn. We do not have to be afraid of future changes. With changes, we can see more outside our comfort zone.

4 To sum up, for all these reasons, I think changes are an inevitable process. We should be glad that there are changes in our life. Changes will only make our life better.

作文中譯加解析

　　我們已備鼓勵留在舒適圈以及避免改變，但是我們必須從虛擬世界中拉回。畢竟，我們每天面對著改變，從我們學生時期到我們工作。改變是不可避免的。你的看法是?改變是不可避免的是真的嗎?

1 我們大多數的人都知道不願意改變是不好的。這將會成為我們生活的阻力。改變將會使我們生活更好。

- 首段指出我們大多數的人都知道不願意改變是不好的。並說明改變將會使我們生活更好。

2 在我們的生活中，從求學時期到我們的工作，我們都將遭遇到改變。不管我們選擇維持不變或我們選擇改變，我們終究必須改變。我們必須適應不斷改變的環境。成為一個不願去改變的人較不可能成為一個具競爭力的人。我們不可能讓我們的環境去適應我們的需求。

- 第二段說明生活中我們勢必會遇到改變，最後更指出一個現實問題，我們必須適應不斷改變的環境。我們不可能讓我們的環境去適應我們的需求。

3 在學校，我們不可能從不同的學科中挑老師。我們告訴校長我們比較喜歡某個美術老師，以致於我們應該要有老師互換計劃。在工作中，不可能要求新的主管改變他們的管理風格來迎合我們。此外，即使你是老闆，你也不可能不斷地改變下屬跟管理者。當然，老闆

249

完全有權力這樣做,但通常公司並非這樣經營的。因此,我們必須面對改變。我們必須經歷改變所以我們才能從那些改變中學習。一位新的主管,即使不同於前任主管,仍有一些額外、值得我們學習的地方。我們不該害怕未來的改變。有了這些改變,我們能夠在舒適圈外看到更多。

- 第三段由學校中舉例我們不可能去挑我們喜歡的老師,而在工作中更不可能要求新的主管改變他們的管理風格來迎合我們。最後指出我們必須面對改變。我們必須經歷改變所以我們才能從那些改變中學習。而且有了這些改變,我們能夠在舒適圈外看到更多。

4 總之,基於這些理由,我認為改變是不可避免的過程,我們都該慶幸生活中有改變。改變只會讓我們生活更好。

- 最後表達自己的看法說明是贊成生活是需要有改變的,而改變只會讓我們生活更好。

字彙補一補

1. hindrance **n.** 阻力
   There is always some hindrance in our life
   我們生活中總是會有些阻力。

2. encounter **v.** 遭遇
   We are going to encounter more obstacles if we do not follow the instruction.
   如果我們不遵照指示，我們會面臨更多障礙。

3. exchanged **adj.** 交換的
   There is an exchanged program in our school.
   我們學校有互換計劃。

4. constantly **adv.** 不斷地
   Technology devises are constantly changed.
   科技裝置不斷地在改變。

5. different **adj.** 不同的
   This is a totally different experience.
   這是全然不同的體驗。

6. inevitable **adv.** 無可避免地
   This is an inevitable process.
   這是不可避免的過程。

Unit 15
Unit 16
Unit 17
Unit 18
Unit 19
Unit 20
Unit 21
Unit 22
Unit 23
Unit 24
Unit 25
Unit 26
Unit 27
Unit 28

重點解析

1. A new executive, even though different from the previous one, can still have something extra, something worth-learning for us to learn.

   一位新的主管，即使不同於前任主管，仍有一些額外、值得我們學習的地方。

   - even though 表示即使…，引導副詞子句，其句型為 even though+S+V，S+V（主要子句），A new executive can still have something extra, something worth-learning for us to learn 為主要子句。
   - is different from 表示不同於…。
   - can still have something extra, something worth-learning for us to learn 表示仍有一些額外、值得我們學習的地方。

2. There is no way that our environments adapt themselves to meet with our requirement.

   我們不可能讓我們的環境去適應我們的需求。

   - adapt to 表示適應或改編…。
   - meet with our requirement 表示符合我們的需求。
   - There is/there are 為常用的基本句型，其句型後常接代名詞或名詞，再加上時間或地點。

3. With changes, we can see more outside our comfort zone.

有了這些改變，我們能夠在舒適圈外看到更多。

- with 為介詞，with changes 表示隨著改變⋯。
- comfort zone 表示舒適圈。
- see 為感官動詞。
- see more outside our comfort zone 看到我們舒適圈外的。

Unit 25

be opposed to Ving 反對…

 可以這樣寫

1. Most girls are opposed to dating an eye broccoli who are in their fifties.

   大部分的女孩反對與 50 幾歲其貌不揚的人約會。

2. A model who are used to socializing with an eye candy is opposed to socializing with an eye broccoli.

   慣於與具賞心悅目容貌的人社交的模特兒反對跟其貌不揚的人打交道。

句型小貼士

- 動名詞的使用用法極廣，具名詞的性質，與不定詞不同其後加 Ving，為常見句型。

- be opposed to 反對…為動名詞慣用語，其後加 Ving。

- eye broccoli 字面上為不具吸引力，引申為其貌不揚的意思。

【⚡】 句型腦激盪

★Most people are opposed to working with a rotten apple.

⇨ Most people are opposed to working with a rotten apple with bad intention.

大部分的人反對與意圖不良的老鼠屎合作。

★Most men are not opposed to dating an eye candy.

⇨ Most men are not opposed to dating an eye candy with no brain.

大部分的男人都不反對與賞心悅目卻無腦的人約會。

★Most girls are not opposed to dating a businessman.

⇨ Most girls are not opposed to dating a successful business-man.

大部分的女孩不反對與成功的商業人士約會。

★Most companies are not opposed to hiring an accountant.

⇨ Most companies are not opposed to hiring a careful accoun-tant.

大部分的公司不反對僱用細心的會計。

★Most dealers are opposed to cooperating a publisher.

⇨ Most dealers are opposed to cooperating a great publisher.

大部分的交易商不反對與出色的出版商合作。

★Most designers are opposed to hiring the cynosure.

⇨ Most designers are opposed to hiring the cynosure who does not like the attention.

大部分的設計師反對僱用不愛受注目的眾所矚目的焦點。

★Most people are not opposed to working in a company.

⇨Most people are not opposed to working in a long-lasting company.

大部分的人不反對在發展長遠的公司工作。

★Most girls are opposed to dating an eye broccoli.

⇨Most girls are opposed to dating an eye broccoli in his late fifties.

大部分的女孩反對與 50 幾歲其貌不揚的人約會。

★Most housewives are not opposed to having a guest over.

⇨Most housewives are not opposed to having a welcomed guest over.

大部分的家庭主婦不反對邀請受歡迎的客戶到家中。

★Most bosses are opposed to hiring an outstanding editor.

⇨Most bosses are opposed to hiring an outstanding editor who is not a team player.

大部分的老闆反對僱用不具團隊合作的出色的編輯。

Instagram PO文小練習

🪐 Tips：opposed to 後面要加上名詞或是 Ving，跟 looking forward to 的用法相同。

_____ is/are opposed to _____

_____

作文範例

/////////////

There is a concern for most educators that kids start learning a foreign language (English) in primary school 1th grade, and there has been a debate for most scholars about whether kids should start learning a foreign language (English) so early. What is your opinion about it?

1 Ages at which kids begin to learn a foreign language have been debated. However, there is a concern for most of us even if we are not teachers or parents. Which is really the best for our future generations?

2 Of course, there are lots of advantages of learning a foreign language, especially a dominant one. We have been educated to at least master a second foreign to find a job. We have to study English as our foreign language since high school. Nowadays, it is even earlier. Kids have to learn English even in primary schools 1st grade.

3 Foreigners of mine are astonished at how early we start to learn English and how much time and efforts most parents and teachers spend or make for us. It is true that it is too early. Most kids are just starting to learn their mother tongue. It is an age where they are vulnerable to learn things. It is also like learning two languages at the same time, while still struggling to learn both of them. Some are still miswriting the Chinese characters and have not had a foundation for Chinese. They are still trying the emulate how to write each Chinese character. Most of the characters still look unintelligible for an adult, but they are moving on to learn a foreign. It just does not make sense. They should learn a foreign until they already have a foundation for their mother tongue. The perfect time for them is probably high school.

4 To sum up, it confounds me why so many educators are in such a rush that they want kids to start learning a foreign language even in the primary school. Even though I love English more than a lot of people, I am opposed to letting our kids learn English at such an early age.

作文中譯加解析

　　大多數教育家對於小孩於小學一年級就開始學習外語（英語）有顧慮，而大多數的學者爭論小孩是否應該這麼早就學習外語（英語）。你的看法是？

1 小孩開始學習外語的年紀一直有所爭議。然而，對我們大多數的人來說是有所顧慮的，即使我們不是老師或父母。

- 首段指出小孩開始學習外語的年紀一直備受爭議。即使我們不是老師或父母，我們也會顧慮學習外語的年紀該定在哪個年齡層。

2 當然，學習外語有許多優點，尤其是具優勢的語言。我們一直被教育出至少要精通一個第二語言以找到一個工作。自國中後，我們必須學習英語為我們的外語。現今，學習外語的時間甚至更早。小孩甚至於小學一年級開始必須學習英語。

- 第二段說明學習外語有許多優點，尤其是具優勢的語言。而現在學習外語的時間又提早了，小孩甚至於小學一年級開始必須學習英語。這是我們該去省思的。

3 我的外國友人驚呼我們怎麼這麼早就開始學習英語，以及大多數家長和老師對我們所花費的時間跟努力。這的確是太早了。大多數的小孩才剛開始學習他們的母語。這是個他們對於學習東西是很脆弱的年紀。像是同時學習兩個語言，而仍吃力的在學習這兩個語言。有些甚至仍寫錯許多中文字，而且對於中文根基也沒打好。他們仍試著模仿如何寫出每個中文字。大多數的字對成人來說仍難辨識，

259

但他們卻移至學習外語。這是説不通的。他們應該直到對本身母語有基礎後才學習外語。對他們而言,最佳的時間可能是國中。

- 第三段以外國友人的看法為開頭,指出大多數家長和老師對我們於學習外語所花費的時間跟努力,其後更説名同時學習兩個語言所造成的衝突,並提出反思畢竟在中文根基也沒打好。且仍試著模仿如何寫出每個中文字。對於他們在這個時期就學習第二外語這是説不通的。

4 總之,令我困惑的是為什麼許多教育家是如此的著急,他們想要小孩子甚至於國小時就學習外國語言。即使我比很多人更愛英語,我反對讓小孩子在這麼早的時候就學習英語。

- 最後指出困惑的部分並表達自己對於這件事的看法,表明小孩子在國小時就學習外國語言是不恰當的。

字彙補一補

1. advantages **n.** 優點

   One of the Advantages of traveling alone is freedom.

   獨自旅行的優點之一是自由。

2. astonished **adj.** 感到驚訝的

   Sometimes we are astonished at our classmates' performance.

   有時候我們對於同學的表現感到驚訝。

3. vulnerable **adj.** 易受攻擊的

   Our computer is vulnerable to a virus attack, if we are not using the anti-virus software.

   我們的電腦易受到病毒的攻擊，如果我們沒使用防毒軟體的話。

4. struggling **adj.** 掙扎的

   We all have the time when we are struggling to learn a foreign language.

   我們總有掙扎於學習外語的時候。

5. foundation **n.** 基礎

   A solid foundation is very important.

   有堅實的基礎是非常重要的。

6. emulate **v.** 模仿

   We try to emulate the successful people.

   我們嘗試模仿成功的人士。

重點解析

1. Foreigners of mine are astonished at how early we start to learn English and how much time and efforts most parents and teachers spend or make for us.

我的外國友人驚呼我們怎麼這麼早就開始學習英語，以及大多數家長和老師對我們所花費的時間跟努力。

> • are astonished at 表示對…感到驚訝。
> • foreigners of mine 表示我的外國友人。
> • and 為對等連接詞連接 how early we start to learn English 和 how much time and efforts most parents and teachers spend or make for us，表示怎麼這麼早就開始學習英語，以及大多數家長和老師對我們所花費的時間跟努力。

2. It is also like learning two languages at the same time, while still struggling to learn both of them.

像是同時學習兩個語言，而仍吃力的在學習這兩個語言。

> • It is also like 表示這也像是…。
> • at the same time 表示同時。
> • while 引導副詞子句，其句型為 while+S+V，S+V(主要子句)，It is also like learning two languages at the same time 為主要子句。
> • are struggling to 表示掙扎…。

3. Most of the characters still look unintelligible for an adult, but they are moving on to learn a foreign.

大多數的字對成人來說仍難辨識，但他們卻移至學習外語。

- Look 為連綴動詞其後加形容詞。
- But 為對等連接詞表示語氣轉折。
- Most of the characters still look unintelligible for an adult 表示大多數的字對成人來說仍難辨識。
- they are moving on to learn a foreign 表示但他們卻移至學習外語。

almost like
幾乎像是

 可以這樣寫

1. It is almost like having a butterfly in my stomach.

   幾乎像是心裡有種七上八下的感覺。

2. Before delivering a speech, everyone seems so quiet and it's like having a butterfly in the stomach.

   發表演說前,每個人似乎都很沉靜,幾乎像是心裡有種七上八下的感覺。

句型小貼士

- 比較級使用用法極廣,包含了原級、比較級和最高級。

- Almost 為修飾原級的程度副詞,其它的有 just、nearly、almost 等。

- a butterfly in my stomach 字面上為為裡面有隻蝴蝶,其引申為緊張或心裡感到七上八下的意思。

句型腦激盪

★It is almost like getting a bonus.
⇨It is almost like getting a bonus for the first time.
　幾乎像是第一次獲取獎金。

★It is almost like getting promoted to the highest position.
⇨It is almost like getting promoted to the highest position.
　幾乎像是升職到最高的職位。

★It is almost like earning a degree.
⇨It is almost like earning a degree with little effort.
　幾乎像是只花一些努力就拿到學位。

★It is almost like getting the present.
⇨It is almost like getting the present for the anniversary.
　幾乎像是結婚週年紀念日拿到禮物。

★It is almost like getting married.
⇨It is almost like getting married in one day.
　幾乎像是一天內完婚。

★It is almost like pursuing a girl.
⇨It is almost like pursuing a girl who is an eye candy.
　幾乎像是追求賞心悅目的女孩。

★It is almost like having swimming in a pool.
⇨It is almost like having swimming in a pool but naked.
　幾乎像是在泳池游泳可是卻裸身。

★It is almost like having a birthday party.

⇨It is almost like having a birthday party in the five star hotel.
幾乎像是在七星級旅館裡過生日派對。

★It is almost like kissing your first love.

⇨It is almost like kissing your first love under the moonlit night.
幾乎像是在月光下親吻初戀情人。

★It is almost like enjoying your ice cream.

⇨It is almost like enjoying your ice cream in the heated desert.
幾乎像是在炎熱的沙漠中享用冰淇淋。

Instagram PO文小練習

✾ Tips：就像是什麼呢？請在 PO 文中再多寫一相關的訊息，例如地點、或是時間等。

It is almost like _____

_____

作文範例

It seems that after announcing that students doing unpaid community service will get extra points when applying for high schools, parents are now a big fan of this act. Some even claim that it should be a mandatory in school programs rather than just a way to get points when applying for high schools.

1 Some people believe that unpaid community service should be a compulsory part of high school programs. It is true that most of people who are in need of help will feel greatly relieved and thankful, but should unpaid community service be mandatory in high school?

2 People do have a concern that this service is related to a charitable act, and why should a charitable act be mandatory? It should be out of people's own will. Those who are in need can genuinely feel that others are really there for them even if it's a simple gesture.

3 Moreover, unpaid community services have been misused in several ways. Since it is mandatory, some students are reluctant to do those chores. They think they should be having fun on Sunday morning or afternoon, not in the hospital

267

cleaning whatever smelly. Also, unpaid community services have become a way for most students to apply for better high schools and universities, but this kind act has lost its meaning. Students in fact have not shown the slightest interests in helping others. They just want to get things done and ask those in charge for signature; otherwise, it will affect their application.

4 To sum up, it is true that doing those services are almost like a plus for teenagers, but the kind gesture has lost its meanings. For all these reasons, I do think unpaid community service should not be a compulsory part of high school programs. It should be something that people do out of their own will.

作文中譯加解析

在宣布學生做無酬的社區服務能於申請高中時得到額外加分後，父母現在都贊同這個舉動。有些甚至主張，無酬的社區服務應該是學校課程的必修課，而非只是於申請學校時加分的手段。

1 有些人認為無酬的社區服務應該是中學課程的必修部分。而大多數真的有需要幫助的人會覺得如釋重負且感到感恩，但是無酬的社區服務真的該是中學的必修嗎？

- 首段指出有些人對於無酬的社區服務的看法，最後提出反問無酬的社區服務真的該是中學的必修嗎？

2 人們真的擔憂此服務與慈善行為有關，但為什麼慈善行為要是必修呢？它應該是出於人們意願。對於那些真的需要幫助的人來說，也能感受到那些人是真的想幫助他們，即使是很微不足道的事。

- 第二段説明人的擔憂但也提出質疑指出但為什麼慈善行為要是必修呢？，畢竟這應該是出於人們意願，即使我們平常做些很微不足道的事但只要是出於自己意願且真心想幫助人，那才真的是慈善行為。

3 此外，無酬的社區服務已於幾個方式中被濫用了。既然是必修的，有些學生不情願去做那些雜事。他們認為他們應該在星期日早晨或下午享受樂趣，而非在醫院清理這些會發出惡臭的東西。而且，無酬的社區服務已成了大多數學生申請更好高中或大學的方式，但是這個善舉卻完全失去意義了。學生事實上對幫助別人毫無興趣。他們想要快點把事情完成，要求那些掌管者簽名，否則會影響他們的申請。

- 第三段指出無酬的社區服務已被濫用了。並舉例出學生們對於作慈善服務的態度，這不該淪為大多數學生申請更好高中或大學的方式，這全然失去意義。

4 總之，對青少年而言，做這些服務幾乎像是很大的幫助，但是這個善舉已失去意義。基於這些理由，我認為無酬的社區服務不該是高中課程的必修部分。它應該是出於人們意願。

- 最後說明此舉已失去意義並表達出看法和立場，說明它應該是出於人們意願。無酬的社區服務不該是高中課程的必修部分。

字彙補一補

1. compulsory **adj.** 義務的
Compulsory education is very important for a nation's growth.
義務教育對於一個國家的成長是非常重要的。

2. genuinely **adv.** 真實地
We genuinely feel that the candidate really want this position.
我們真摯地感受到候選人真的想要這個職位。

3. unpaid **adj.** 無酬的
Although this is unpaid, we really enjoy doing it.
儘管這是無酬的,我們真的很喜愛做這個。

4. smelly **adj.** 惡臭的
The kitchen is really smelly.
廚房真的很臭。

5. signature **n.** 簽名
A signature represents a person's style.
簽名代表著個人風格。

6. teenager **n.** 青少年
Sometimes teenagers may exhibit rebellious behavior.
有時候青少年可能會表現出叛逆的行為。

重點解析

1. Those who are in need can genuinely feel that others are really there for them even if it's a simple gesture.

對於那些真的需要幫助的人來說，也能感受到那些人是真的想幫助他們，即使是很微不足道的事。

- Even if…表示條件句引導一副詞子句，為 if+S+V 的句型。
- even if it's a simple gesture 表示即使是很微不足道的事。
- can genuinely feel that others are really there for them 表示也能感受到那些人是真的想幫助他們。
- who 引導關係代名詞子句，句中為 who are in need 表示受需求。

2. Also, unpaid community services have become a way for most students to apply for better high schools and universities, but the kind act has lost its meaning.

此外，無酬的社區服務已於幾個方式中被濫用了。

- also 表示而且。
- have become 為現在完成式表示已經成為…。
- apply for 表示申請…。
- but 為對等連接詞表示轉折，此為 but the kind act has lost its meaning 表示此善舉已失去其意義。

3. They just want to get things done and ask those in charge for signature; otherwise, it will affect their application.

他們想要快點把事情完成，要求那些掌管者簽名，否則會影響他們的申請。

- otherwise 表示否則。
- They just want to get things done 表示他們只想要事情快點完成。
- be in charge 表示…為…人所負責或掌控。
- it will affect their application 表示會影響他們申請。

I don't think
我不認為

可以這樣寫

///////////

1. I don't think they are neck and neck.
   我不認為他們並駕齊驅。

2. I don't think it's that simple.
   我不認為有這麼簡單。

句型小貼士

- Think 的用法極廣,可以當不及物動詞和及物動詞,其後常加上 that 子句。

- I don't think 表示我不認為…,表達自己對事物否定的看法。

- Neck and neck 只在競賽或比賽中兩人不相上下、並駕齊驅。

句型腦激盪

★I don't think he will be promoted.
⇨I don't think he will be promoted in such a short time.
我不認為他在這麼短的時間內會升遷。

★I don't think she will get fired.
⇨I don't think she will immediately get fired.
我不認為她立刻會被解雇。

★I don't think they will be awarded.
⇨I don't think they will be awarded, after all there're too many capable competitors in this game.
我不認為他們會獲獎，畢竟這場競賽中有太多有實力的競爭者了。

★I don't think he will be sanctioned.
⇨I don't think he will be sanctioned so soon.
我不認為他這麼快會受到制裁。

★I don't think she will feel satisfied.
⇨I don't think she will feel satisfied with the result.
我不認為她對這個結果感到滿意。

★I don't think he is expecting to see that.
⇨I don't really think he is expecting to see that.
我不認為他期待看到這個。

★I don't think she is afraid.
⇨I don't think she is afraid of stepping on the scale.
我不認為她害怕站在秤上。

★I don't think they are wasting their time.

⇨I don't think they are wasting their time, on the contrary, they are trying to get more time for their team.

我不認為他們是在浪費他們時間，反而是在試著為他們隊伍爭取更多的時間。

★I don't think she will approve.

⇨I don't think she will approve of his decision.

我不認為她會同意他的選擇。

★I don't think she will sign.

⇨I don't think she will sign the contract.

我不認為她會簽這份合約。

Instagram PO文小練習

💠 Tips：I don't think 後面只要簡單的接上一個子句就完成囉。有什麼你不這麼認為的事嗎？

I don't think _____

_____

作文範例

Government officials used to think that with more sports facilities being built, this will improve overall public health, but this has never been the case. Contrary to public beliefs, most facilities remain either disused or randomly used.

1 Increasing the number of sports facilities will have a little effect on public health because the point is whether people are willing to exercise or not. If people are unwilling to exercise, what is the point of increasing more sports facilities?

2 From the big question mark here, it seems that other measures need to be taken to improve public health. First, we have to think why few people are willing to exercise and by any chance will use the newly-increased facilities to exercise so that the goal of improving the public health can be reached.

3 Nowadays, there is a lack of the awareness that people should exercise more. Governments should educate their citizens that exercising is important, and they should hold as many exercise-related activities as possible. Furthermore, health and nutrition should be the required course in the primary school and high school so that people can have a thorough understanding about how to eat and how to have a healthy lifestyle. Also, governments should impose tax on junk foods so that the goal of improving public health can be reached.

4 There are several nations that have already charged extra fees for those companies who produce junk foods. This is certainly a milestone for us simply because if all foods are bland and contain less fat and sugar, there is no way that people can gain such alarming weight in a single week. Diet pills companies are no longer able to make a fortune from us.

5 To sum up, it is obvious that <u>people do not think</u> it is wise to build sports facilities, and for all the reasons, other measures need to be taken so that the goal of improving the overall public health is probable, but improving the number of sports facilities will not work.

作文中譯加解析

　　政府官員以前認為隨著更多的運動設施的建立，會改進整體大眾健康，但實際上卻不是這回事。與大眾思考相反的是，大多數的設施仍舊無人使用或很少人使用。

1 增加運動設施的數量對大眾健康有很小的影響，因為重點是人們是否有意願去運動。如果人們沒有意願去運動，那麼增加更多的運動設施的目的在哪呢？

- 首段提出反思因為重點是人們是否有意願去運動。並提出反問如果人們沒有意願去運動，那麼增加更多的運動設施的目的在哪呢?這才是值得我們去思考的。

2 從這個大問題，似乎需要採取其他的措施來改進大眾健康。首先，我們必須去思考為什麼有些人不願意去運動，而且可能會偶然的使用新增的設施運動，以至於增進大眾健康的目標可以達到。

- 第二段説明我們必須去思考為什麼有些人不願意去運動，才能進一步了解提升人民運動的意願才能使得民眾更健康，而非從增加運動設施上著手。

3 現今，缺乏人們應該多運動的意識。政府應該教育他們的市民，運動是重要的。他們應該舉辦越多與運動相關的活動。此外，健康和營養應該是小學和中學的必修課程，所以人們能對如何吃和如何有健康的生活方式有透徹的了解。而且，政府應該對垃圾食物課稅，改善大眾健康的目標才能達到。

- 第三段由教育為出發點指出由於人們缺乏多運動的意識。可以從舉辦活動上著手，甚至將健康和營養應該是小學和中學的必修課程，如此人們能對如何吃和如何有健康的生活方式有透徹的了解。政府也可以對垃圾食物課稅。

4 有幾個國家已經有對那些製造垃圾食物的公司索取額外的費用。對我們來說這確實是個里程碑，只因為如果所有食物都很平淡而且有較少的脂肪和糖，人們不可能在一星期內增加如此驚人的體重。減肥藥品公司不再從我們身上賺取大把鈔票。

- 第四段提出有幾個國家已經有對那些製造垃圾食物的公司索取額外的費用。如果人們飲食都很正常更不可能讓減肥藥品公司不再從我們身上賺取大把鈔票。

5 總之，儘管所有的理由，是需要採取其它的措施，所以改進整體大眾的健康的目標是可能的，但是增加運動設施的數量不是有效的。

- 最後總結由其他措施去改進整體大眾的健康的目標是可能的，但是增加運動設施的數量是不可行的。

字彙補一補

1. increasing **adj.** 增加的
Increasing the tax is perhaps not the best solution.
增稅似乎不是最佳的解決之道。

2. unwilling **adj.** 不情願的
He is unwilling to give his friends a ride.
他不情願載他朋友一程。

3. measure **n.** 措施
Measures need to be taken to solve traffic jam problems.
須採取措施已解決交通擁擠的問題。

4. educate **v.** 教育
We need to educate our kids so that they will be well-behaved.
我們需要教育我們的小孩所以他們才能表現得體。

5. thorough **adj.** 徹底的
A thorough understanding is a must, especially in a logical thinking task.
徹底的了解是必要的,尤其是在邏輯思考的任務裡。

6. milestone **n.** 里程碑
This is certainly a milestone for most of us.
對我們來說這確實是個里程碑。

重點解析

1. Increasing the number of sports facilities will have a little effect on public health because the point is whether people are willing to exercise or not.

   增加運動設施的數量對大眾健康有很小的影響，因為重點是人們是否有意願去運動。

   - increasing the number of sports facilities 為動名詞當主詞…。
   - the number of sports facilities 表示數量。
   - have a little effect 表示有些許影響，介系詞加 on。
   - because 表示因為…，引導副詞子句，其句型為 because+S+V，S+V（主要子句），Increasing the number of sports facilities will have a little effect on public health 為主要子句。
   - whether people are willing to exercise or not.不論人們是否願意運動。

2. First, we have to think why few people are willing to exercise and by any chance will use the newly-increased facilities to exercise so that the goal of improving the public health can be reached.

   首先，我們必須去思考為什麼有些人不願意去運動，而且可能會偶然的使用新增的設施運動，以至於增進大眾健康的目標可以達到。

   - are willing to 表示願意…。
   - by any chance…表示偶然機會之下。
   - so that 表示如此…以致於。

• the goal of improving the public health can be reached，才能達到改善大眾健康的目標。

3. This is certainly a milestone for us simply because if all foods are bland and contain less fat and sugar, there is no way that people can gain such alarming weight in a single week.

對我們來説這確實是個里程碑，只因為如果所有食物都很平淡而且有較少的脂肪和糖，人們不可能在一星期內增加如此驚人的體重。

• if…表示條件句引導一副詞子句，為 if+S+V 的句型。
• if all foods are bland and contain less fat and sugar 表示如果所有食物都很平淡而且有較少的脂肪和糖。
• there is 為常用的基本句型，其句型後常接代名詞或名詞，再加上時間或地點。
• gain such alarming weight in a single week 表示在一星期內增加如此驚人的體重。

on second thought
進一步考慮後

可以這樣寫

/////////////

1. On second thought, she buys a fake LV bag for her sister.

   進一步考慮後，她買了仿冒的 LV 包包給她姐姐。

2. On second thought, he bought some gelato for his friends down the Pearl Street.

   進一步考慮後，他在珍珠街的盡頭買了一些義式冰淇淋給他朋友。

句型小貼士

- buy 的用法極廣，常用句型為 buy sth for sb。

- buy 為授與動詞，同類的詞有 choose, make, order, bring, grant, hand, tell, show, tell, write 等等，授與動詞加直接受詞後再加上介系詞和間接受詞，常用句型為授與動詞+DO+介系詞+IO。

- on second thought 表示進一步考慮後，於對話中常出現。

句型腦激盪

★On second thought, she buys a satchel for her sister.
⇨On second thought, she buys a black satchel for her sister.
進一步考慮後，她買了黑色的小提包給她姐姐。

★On second thought, she bought a purple purse.
⇨On second thought, she bought a purple purse with her name inscribed on it.
進一步考慮後，她買了烙著她名字的紫色錢包。

★On second thought, john buys a house.
⇨On second thought, john buys a house near the lake.
進一步考慮後，約翰買了鄰近湖邊的小屋。

★On second thought, she chose to stay in an island.
⇨On second thought, she chose to stay in an island with pristine forests.
進一步考慮後，她選擇待在有原始森林的島上。

★On second thought, she buys her birthday present.
⇨On second thought, she buys a yacht for her birthday present.
進一步考慮後，她買了遊艇當作她生日禮物。

★On second thought, she books a plane ticket.
⇨On second thought, she books a plane ticket to New Zealand.
進一步考慮後，她訂了去紐西蘭的機票。

★On second thought, she buys a book.

⇨On second thought, she buys a book for the further reference.

　進一步考慮後，她買了書作進一步參考。

★On second thought, he buys a pencil for the test.

⇨On second thought, he buys a 2B pencil for the test.

　進一步考慮後，他為了考試買了 2B 鉛筆。

★On second thought, she buys a pink sofa.

⇨On second thought, she buys a pink sofa that matches perfectly with the living room.

　進一步考慮後，她買了跟客廳很相襯的粉紅色沙發。

★On second thought, they buy pearl milk tea.

⇨On second thought, they buy pearl milk tea with ice.

　進一步考慮後，他們買了加冰的珍珠奶茶。

💬 **Instagram PO文小練習**

⚛ Tips：在美式英文中寫作 On second thought，而在英式英文中則寫作 On second thoughts，這裡的 thought 是複數名詞，你注意到了嗎？

On second thought, _____

_____

作文範例

/////////

The disappearance of languages has been a huge concern for many nations. The relevance between languages and our life cannot be overstressed. Is it really true that we only have to speak a few languages if there are fewer languages exist, and do not have to make an effort to preserve dead languages?.

1 The disappearance of languages hinges on several factors, but powerful nations tend to have the total control that certain languages are commonly used and particular languages are less frequently used. It may seem irrelevant to us that every year several languages die out and life will be a lot easier if there are few languages in the world. All the above statements have led us to rethink this issue.

2 Nowadays, we speak the dominant language, mainly English and Chinese. There is no such thing that we should speak few dead languages which are about to die out or are already dead. Therefore, even if several languages are dying out, we still have to speak several dominant languages. It totally has nothing to do with whether life will be easier if there are few languages in the world, but there is still a need for us to preserve those languages from dying out.

3 Even if we do not have to speak minority languages, every human language is still the heritage of the human race. Cultural diversity is lost when a language dies. Cultural diversity and language diversity are conducive to the development and the survival of the human race. The survival of culture is heavily dependent on languages. The connection between cultures and languages cannot be overlooked. Thus, maintaining as many as languages is important. Our life will not be easier if there are only few languages.

4 To sum up, the numbers of languages have a lot to do with our life. On second thought, we simply cannot say it is irrelevant to our life. Most important of all, we still have to speak several dominant languages, even if several languages are dying out.

作文中譯加解析

　　語言消失一直是許多國家非常關注的事情。語言和我們生活的關聯性的重要性更是不言而喻。我們僅需說少數幾種語言,如果只有較少的語言存在,而且不用做出努力去保存死語言,這是真的嗎?

1 語言消失是取決於幾個因素,但是強國傾向於對特定語言是否普遍使用或特定語言較少使用有著絕對的控制權。每年有幾個語言消失可能對我們來說,似乎毫無相關,且生活會因為較少語言的存在而變得更為容易。而以上的這些陳述也引領我們去重新思考這個議題。

- 首段語言消失是取決於幾個因素,語言消失看似與我們毫無關連,但這個議題卻與我們息息相關,強國對於特定語言的使用的確導致了某些語言的消失。

2 現今,我們說著優勢語言,主要是英文和中文。關於我們應該說即將消失的語言或已經消失的語言的事是不可能發生的。因此,即使有些語言正面臨滅絕,我們仍必須說幾個優勢語言。這完全與生活是否會因此而變得簡單無關,但是仍有我們該保護那些語言免於滅絕的需求在。

- 第二段提出說明並反思,即使有些語言正面臨滅絕,我們仍必須說幾個優勢語言才能在競爭社會中生存,我們的生活並不會因為某些語言的消失而變得更輕鬆。

3　即使我們不需要説少數語言，每個人類語言仍然是人類的遺產。當語言死亡後，文化的多樣性將消失。文化多樣性和語言多樣性有益於人類生存和發展。文化的存續也極仰賴語言。語言和文化是不能被忽視的。因此，能維持越多語言是重要的。我們的生活也不會因為只有少數幾個語言而變得更簡單。

- 第三段指出每個人類語言仍然是人類的遺產。也指出語言與文化多樣性的關連性，畢竟文化多樣性和語言多樣性有益於人類生存和發展。文化的存續也極仰賴語言。語言和文化是不能被忽視的。

4　語言數量的多寡與我們生活息息相關。我們無法簡單地説這與我們生活無關。最重要的是，我們仍然必須説幾個優勢語言，即使幾個語言正在消失。

- 最後以 to sum up 做結尾，説明語言數量的多寡與我們生活息息相關。現實是即使幾個語言正在消失，我們仍然必須説幾個優勢語言。

字彙補一補

1. disappearance **n.** 消失

The disappearance of bees may have a lot to do with pesticide use.

蜜蜂的消失可能與殺蟲劑的使用息息相關。

2. dependent **adj.** 依賴的

Kids are entirely dependent on their parents.

小孩子全然地依賴他們的父母。

3. diversity **n.** 多樣性

Product diversity is an important factor for alluring customers.

產品的多樣性是吸引顧客的重要因素。

4. commonly **adv.** 普遍地

Now some lotions are commonly used in every household.

現在有些乳液於每個家庭中普遍地使用。

5. frequently **adv.** 頻繁地

John is said to be the one who frequently changes his girlfriend.

據說約翰是個頻繁換女友的人。

6. dominant **adj.** 占優勢的

Dominant languages are used by many people.

優勢語言為許多人使用。

重點解析

1. The disappearance of languages hinges on several factors, but powerful nations tend to have the total control that certain languages are commonly used and particular languages are less frequently used.

語言消失是取決於幾個因素，但是強國傾向於對特定語言是否普遍使用或特定語言較少使用有著絕對的控制權。

> - The disappearance of languages 表示語言的消失。
> - hinges on several factors 表示取決於幾個因素。
> - but 為對等連接詞表示語氣轉折。
> - have the total control 表示具有絕對的掌控。
> - tend to 表示傾向於…。
> - commonly used 表示普遍地使用，less frequently used 表示較少使用。

2. It may seem irrelevant to us that every year several languages die out and life will be a lot easier if there are few languages in the world.

每年有幾個語言消失可能對我們來說，似乎毫無相關，且生活會因為較少語言的存在而變得更為容易。

> - It may seem irrelevant to us 表示可能對我們來說試無關的。
> - die out 表示滅絕。
> - there are 為常用的基本句型，其句型後常接代名詞或名詞，再加上時間或地點。
> - if…表示條件句引導一副詞子句，為 if+S+V 的句型。

- if there are few languages in the world 表示世界上只有幾種語言。

3. Cultural diversity and language diversity are conducive to the development and the survival of the human race.

文化多樣性和語言多樣性有益於人類生存和發展。

- cultural diversity 表示文化多樣性，language diversity 表示語言多樣性。
- are conducive to 表示有益於…。
- are conducive to the development and the survival of the human race 表示有益於人類生存和發展。

Learn Smart! 048

每日一句的 Instagram PO 文，輕鬆學好英文寫作

作　　者　韋爾
封面構成　高鍾琪
內頁構成　菩薩蠻數位文化有限公司

發 行 人　周瑞德
企劃編輯　陳欣慧
校　　對　陳韋佑、饒美君
印　　製　大亞彩色印刷製版股份有限公司
初　　版　2015 年 07 月
定　　價　新台幣 349 元
出　　版　倍斯特出版事業有限公司
電　　話　(02) 2351-2007
傳　　真　(02) 2351-0887
地　　址　100 台北市中正區福州街 1 號 10 樓之 2
E - m a i l　best.books.service@gmail.com

港澳地區總經銷　泛華發行代理有限公司
地址　香港新界將軍澳工業邨駿昌街 7 號 2 樓
電話　(852) 2798-2323
傳真　(852) 2796-5471

國家圖書館出版品預行編目(CIP)資料

每日一句的 Instagram PO 文,輕鬆學好英文寫作 /
韋爾著. -- 初版. -- 臺北市 ： 倍斯特, 2015.07
　面 ；　公分. -- (Learn smart! ; 48)
　ISBN 978-986-91915-1-7(平裝)

　1.英語　2.寫作法

805.　　　　　　　　　　　　17104010924